Lost Souls

Jacqueline E. Smith

Wind Trail Publishing

Lost Souls

Wind Trail Publishing
PO Box 830851
Richardson, TX 75083-0851
www.WindTrailPublishing.com

Second Paperback Edition, April 2020

ISBN-13: 978-0-9972450-9-7
ISBN-10: 0-9972450-9-3

Cover Design: Wind Trail Publishing

This is a work of fiction. Characters, places, and incidents portrayed in
this novel are either products of the author's imagination or used
fictitiously.

For the love of my life, Matthew Gray Gubler.
Yes, I will marry you.

"When a man's soul is certainly in hell, his body will scarce lie quiet in a tomb however costly…"

Robert Louis Stevenson

CHAPTER ONE

"*The question that I get asked the most, surprisingly, isn't 'Can you do a reading for me?' or 'How often do you see them?' It's 'Do they scare you?'*

"*The honest answer to that question is yes, but not for the reasons that you'd probably imagine.*

"*Seeing ghosts isn't like M. Night Shyamalan or Stephen King would have you believe. They're not disfigured or bloodied or mangled. They're not even transparent. They look like you and me.*

"*What scares me isn't the idea that these people are dead, or that they tend to appear when I least expect it, although I'll admit, that does get old. It isn't even the fact that these spirits often possess psychic abilities that most living human beings do not. No, what's always scared me is the idea that I'm different, that I'm not like everybody else.*

"*Even though it makes total sense, it looks ridiculous when I put it down on paper. But it's true. I'm terrified of what seeing ghosts makes me, especially in the eyes of the people around me, most of all in eyes of the people I love.*

"*When you're a kid, you learn fairly quickly how the world treats the outcast, the weirdo, the reject. You may not want to be the person that society turns their back on, but you definitely do not want to be the person that they single out. That's even worse than being ignored, in my experience. And that's why I tried my best to remain invisible, to keep my secret for all those years. I was terrified, not of the ghosts, but of what other people might think of me, Michael Sinclair, the guy who can see the ghosts.*"

It wasn't the passage that Michael would have chosen to read, but it seemed to be everybody's favorite, so it was the one that talk-show host Jack Landon had selected. After all, he was just thankful that his book, *Seeing Ghosts*, was getting

1

the publicity that it was. It wasn't always easy for a first-time author, but as Luke had reminded him in the midst of the publishing process, "It's all about who you know."

That was probably why his book had been released so quickly. Luke had put him in touch with his publisher before Michael had even finished drafting the outline. They drew him up a contract less than a week later. Michael didn't have a whole lot of experience in the publishing world, none for that matter, but he had a sneaking suspicion that most book deals didn't happen that quickly.

Being best friends with ghost-hunting superstar Luke Rainer probably had something to do with that.

In the two months since the book had been published, it had soared to the top of several non-fiction bestsellers lists. True, there were more than a few critics out there calling the book "simply ridiculous," "catastrophically outrageous," and "absolute rubbish," but most of the feedback he'd received from readers had been positive. And, as Luke and Kate had both reminded him, that was what mattered. He'd written the book to help people, to tell them the truth, to offer them some sort of reassurance that life didn't end with death.

Of course, the six-figure advance didn't hurt either.

Michael knew that if he had been any other first-time author, he would have had to search much longer for a deal, and when and *if* he did manage to land one, he doubted it would have been for the amount of money that Luke's publisher had offered him. He would also soon begin earning royalties from the book and he received a check for every public appearance he made in a bookstore or on television.

For the first time in his life, Michael had more money than he knew what to do with. It was a stark contrast to the way he'd been living for the past year. Really, to the way he'd been living most of his twenty-eight years. But he'd been able to adjust fairly quickly. He helped his mother pay off her house so she could finally retire. He traded in his old car for a slightly used but still relatively new Volvo.

And he'd found the perfect engagement ring for Kate.

Brink had helped him pick it out, which, in retrospect, may not have been the best idea. After all, he and Brink had never exactly seen eye-to-eye when it came to romance or fashion. The second they walked into the first jewelry store, Brink zeroed in on a glitzy, gaudy clunker of a ring. Michael grimaced.

"What? Too expensive?" Brink asked.

"It's ugly," Michael remarked.

"How is that ugly? It's got like fifty diamonds! It's probably the sparkliest ring here!"

"Yeah, which makes it the perfect ring for a magpie, not Kate."

"She does have that demon bird that she really loves," Brink reminded him. "Come on, man. Look, I know you think you're some hot-shot author now, but let's face it. You don't know anything about women."

"What are you talking about? I know something about women. I'm dating a woman."

"Um, Sir?" The salesgirl who'd interrupted him didn't look like she was at all comfortable approaching the crazy man having an argument with himself in the middle of a jewelry store, but at least she was polite about it. "Is there anything I can help you with today?"

"No, we're just looking!" Brink yelled in Michael's ear, as though that would miraculously make the girl able to hear him. Michael tried not to wince.

"Actually, I'm looking for an engagement ring for my girlfriend."

"Really?" Michael didn't think she meant to sound rude, but he had to admit, he couldn't really blame her for being surprised that a woman had stuck around long enough for him to propose marriage.

He had to let the poor girl off the hook.

"Yeah, uh... I really haven't decided on anything yet. Just browsing for now."

3

"Okay, well, if you have any questions, feel free to ask. My name is Amy."

"Thanks."

"Trust me, brother. When it comes to women, you can't go wrong with *bling*," Brink insisted once Amy had moved on to the next customer.

"As much as I appreciate your insight, Brink, I'm going with my instincts on this one. That ring isn't Kate."

"Whatever, man. It's your engagement. But don't blame me when she's not impressed with whatever dinky ring you pick out."

Really, *why* had Michael asked him to come along?

They visited three different stores before Michael finally found the perfect ring. It was simple yet elegant, stylish yet demure: a single diamond in an antique, white gold setting. Beautiful. Classy. Kate.

Now all he had to do was ask her father's permission to propose to her.

It was old-fashioned. He knew that. But he also knew that Kate's late fiancé, Trevor, had done the same thing. It wasn't that Michael was trying to copy Trevor, or that he felt like Kate's former beau had set the standards on proposals. The opposite, in fact. He respected Trevor, and he respected the love that he and Kate had shared. He wanted to honor that respect.

Thankfully, Kate's father, Rex, had always seemed to like him, unlike her mother, who remained convinced that Michael wasn't good for Kate. Michael had never admitted it to Kate, but Terri Avery kind of frightened him. She was so protective of her daughter. It made sense, given that Kate had survived a devastating car crash, incidentally the same one that had killed Trevor.

But he couldn't dwell on any of that now. The commercial break was almost over. Then he would be back on with Jack Landon for the rest of his guest appearance and interview.

"And we're back, ladies and gentlemen. We're talking with Michael Sinclair, the man who can actually see and communicate with the dead *and* who has just written a book which is sitting pretty at the top of non-fiction bestsellers lists across the country," Jack Landon announced. "So, Michael, let's talk about the book. What inspired you, after all these years, to finally tell your story?"

Well, I was broke, unemployed, and really had nothing better to do, was the honest answer to that question, but Luke had warned him that while he and Kate might find Michael's sardonic sense of humor oh so charming, potential book-buyers and readers may not.

"I guess I've finally reached a point where I feel like I'm able to tell it. But you know, I really think that my friends and my family had a lot to do with it. They've kind of helped me to realize that what I can do... well, that it isn't a bad thing. They helped me to understand that I can bring others, both living and deceased, a bit of hope and comfort. And that's really what I wanted to accomplish with the book. I wanted to reassure people that death is not the end."

The audience cheered. A few members sniffled. One lady even whimpered like she was trying not to weep.

"These friends of yours, if you don't mind me asking, are they all still amongst the living?" Jack Landon asked.

"Most of them are," Michael answered with a grin. That got a few laughs.

"I know you go into it a little in your book, but I've just got to ask. What is it like? Going out into the world and knowing that so many of the people that you encounter... are dead?"

"It used to be really unnerving, but like I mentioned in the book, it wasn't because the ghosts were dead. It was because I didn't want to draw attention to myself and when you start interacting with someone that other people can't see... that tends to draw a lot of attention."

Another chuckle from the audience.

"So, you're not afraid of ghosts?"

"I mean, I'm afraid of some ghosts. I'm afraid of the ones who threaten to beat me up or possess my girlfriend. But I'd be afraid of living people threatening that kind of stuff too."

Again, laughter. Man, he was on fire today! People never thought he was funny. Well, the people he hung out with anyway. Luke and Brink just sighed and shook their heads whenever he made a joke or witty comment, and Kate only laughed when he wasn't trying to be funny. Like the day when her stupid bird had attacked him and he'd fallen over her coffee table trying to get away from him.

Oh, Lord. What was it going to be like when they were married? Was Marlon Brando the Demon Conure going to move in with him? Kate loved that bird. There was no way she was going to leave him behind, despite Michael's constant insistence that her precious baby would kill him in his sleep if he got the chance. Of course, Kate just laughed at that, too.

"So, what's next for you? There have been rumors of a reality show in the works."

"Those are absolutely not true," Michael insisted. Though he had a fairly decent idea of where those rumors had originated.

"But is that something that you would consider?" Jack Landon pressed.

"I don't think so."

"Any particular reason?"

There were several reasons, actually. Although Michael had agreed to appear on *Cemetery Tours* with Luke and the crew, he was far from what anyone would call a natural on camera. He was a private person. He liked his personal space. That, and reality shows always just seemed so... fake. To him, anyway. Kate didn't really care for them either and she was a television fanatic. Finally, he couldn't help but feel that a reality television show would mean benefitting from other people's grief. And although he knew there were several good psychics and mediums out there who did participate in reality shows, he just didn't feel it was the right path for him.

Instead of explaining all this to Jack Landon, however, he simply gave the answer that he'd been giving Luke for years. "It's just not really my thing."

"What is your thing?"

Another question that wasn't necessarily easy to answer. For so many years, his "thing" had been ignoring every ghost that wandered his way and putting on a normal facade every time he stepped out in public. Now, he supposed the ghosts were still his thing. But even though he'd accepted it, he didn't want his entire life to be about death.

"This is going to sound so cliché, so please forgive me, but right now, my thing is appreciating the little things. Spending time with my girlfriend. Trying to learn how to cook more than just pasta and microwave meals. Reading more books. I've spent my whole life living in the shadows. Now I'm just trying to figure out how to *live*."

The audience broke into another round of roaring applause. Jack Landon smiled at him.

"Well Michael, it seems to me, and to everyone who has enjoyed your book, that you are well on your way. And I offer you my sincerest congratulations."

"Thank you," Michael grinned.

It was a strange feeling, knowing that for once, everything seemed to be going right. And he almost didn't want to jinx anything by acknowledging it. But he also knew that he couldn't take it for granted. Life *was* good. Better than good.

In that moment, knowing that he would soon be going home to new opportunities, to new adventures, and especially to Kate, life was damn near perfect.

CHAPTER TWO

Flight 109 from LAX to Dallas: Within Range

Six weeks was too long.

Kate was thrilled for Michael. She really was. He'd written an excellent book and he deserved every bit of good fortune that came his way. She understood that touring and signing books and meeting with readers was all part of the new author gig. But *six weeks*? That was long enough to drive a girl crazy.

They'd talked every day, of course. Whenever he had a moment of down time, he'd text her to say hello or to ask her how her day had been. They video-chatted when they could and he always called her to say goodnight. Still, it wasn't the same as actually having him there with her, and even though she was a strong, independent woman who could get along just fine without her man, well... she missed him.

Flight 109 from LAX to Dallas: Arrived

Thankfully, she wouldn't have to miss him for much longer. Mere minutes, if that. Even though Michael had told her she didn't have to pick him up from the airport, she'd insisted that she wanted to. After six weeks, three days, five hours, and forty-three minutes (not that she'd been counting), she wasn't about to wait another second.

Anxious and jittery from excitement and anticipation, Kate tapped her foot and once again, glanced expectantly at the Departures and Arrivals board.

Flight 109 from LAX to Dallas: At Gate

At the same time, her phone chimed.

1 New Message

From: Michael

We're here!

Finally! He was home!

Even though she knew he probably hadn't even made it off the plane yet, Kate began scanning the crowds for her tall, dark, and haunted Prince Charming. It was funny, but in the six weeks he'd been gone, she'd even begun to miss Brink.

Her pounding heart leapt into her throat when she finally spotted him. His dark, messy hair was unkempt and a bit longer than she remembered and he wore comfy jeans and a San Diego t-shirt. He looked sleepy, but younger somehow, and he was happy. Kate could see it in his eyes.

He was especially happy to see her.

Kate couldn't resist. She broke into a sprint and threw herself into his arms.

Home, she sighed, burying her face in his neck and breathing in his familiar scent. She realized then just *how* much she had missed him; his touch, his embrace, his warmth, his comfort. Everything about him was home.

Without saying a word, Kate wrapped her arms around his neck, rose up on her toes, and kissed him. Not a swift, friendly kiss. A kiss for the movies. A kiss for all the kisses that they had missed in the past six weeks. Somewhere in the background, someone catcalled and began to applaud. It was only then that Kate backed down.

Michael, blushing and grinning from ear-to-ear, could only laugh.

"It's good to see you, too," he told her.

"You're never going away for that long again. You got it?"

"I promise," Michael agreed. "And if I do, I'm taking you with me."

"That's more like it," Kate smiled and kissed him again. "So, how was your flight?"

"I don't know. I slept through most of it," Michael confessed as they made their way to baggage claim.

"You probably needed it."

"I know I needed it. I can't wait to sleep in my own bed."

"Well, I hope I can keep you awake for at least a few more hours. I want to take you home, make you dinner, and then shamelessly have my way with you," Kate flirted, wrapping both her arms back around his waist.

"You know, I think I'm okay with that," Michael smiled, his eyes sparkling in spite of the slight shadows surrounding them.

While they waited for his suitcase at the dreadful luggage carousel, Michael entertained Kate with a story about the ghost he'd met in the taxi cab on his way to the airport. This particular ghost was a bit of a prankster. He liked to change the radio stations and mess with passengers' hair and every once in a while, when he could muster up the energy, he'd steal change right out of their pockets. Of course, when he tried that with Michael, Michael looked him straight in the eye and asked what he thought he was doing.

"Oh, I wish I could have seen the look on his face," Kate declared. "Speaking of ghosts, how's Brink?"

"Trying to convince me that we need to move to California," Michael answered as his suitcase finally made it around to where they were standing.

"Why?"

"He says he really found himself there. I think it's all the hipsters."

Kate laughed.

"God, I've missed you," she said, snuggling up to him as they meandered through the crowded airport to the parking lot.

Michael slung his free arm around her shoulders and kissed the top of her head.

"I've missed you more."

Back home at the Riverview Apartment Complex, Kate helped Michael carry his luggage up to his apartment. Then, she scampered back over to her place to retrieve her own bags while he unpacked and changed into something more comfortable. He'd asked her what the dress code was for dinner, which she found super sweet and considerate. He probably would have worn a suit and tie if she'd asked him to, but after his six weeks away and a long day of traveling, she told him that he could wear whatever he wanted.

When she arrived back at his apartment, just across the landing from her own, he was still wearing the same t-shirt, but he had changed out of the jeans and into his favorite pair of cozy, plaid pajama pants. Kate couldn't help but smile. They were the same pajama pants he'd been wearing when they'd met over a year ago, just outside his front door.

"Hey," she smiled. "You kinda look like this guy that I have a huge crush on."

"And you kinda look like my favorite person in the world," he smiled, taking her into his arms. "Oh, I'm sorry. Favorite *living* person."

She giggled.

"Hi, Brink."

"... No," Michael remarked, casting his invisible friend a sidelong glance.

"What is he saying?" Kate wondered.

Michael sighed, obviously debating whether or not to tell her.

"He wants to remind us that there are pure, innocent eyes watching and kindly requests that we keep things PG."

"No promises. Sorry."

"He says in that case, we need to text Gavin and tell him to leave the television on. Oh, and if he asks, Brink's new favorite show is *Game of Thrones*, but he's only just made it to season two, so no spoilers."

"You know, Brink, that's not exactly a show for pure and innocent eyes," Kate reminded him.

"He says he looks away when there are naked people."

"Oh, yeah right," Kate teased. Then she turned back to Michael. "So are we ever getting you back on the *Game of Thrones* bandwagon?" A few months ago, she'd convinced him to sit through a single episode with her. She had had no such luck since. But at least she'd managed to get Brink hooked on George R.R. Martin's epic series.

"It's too much," Michael groaned playfully. "My brain can't handle all the characters and places and weird relationships... And no."

"No what?" Kate asked, wondering what Brink was saying now.

"He says that his birthday is coming up and I should buy him the audiobooks."

"Hey, that's not a bad idea. When's your birthday, Brink?" Kate asked.

"Please don't buy him the audiobooks," Michael pleaded.

"Why not? If it gets him reading, I think it would make a great gift."

"Because he'll have it playing *all* the time and he can't wear headphones which means *I'll* have to listen to it."

"*You* can wear headphones," Kate reminded him. Just then, Michael rolled his eyes, but Kate suspected she wasn't the reason. "What's Brink saying now?"

"That in the event of a divorce, he wants you to have custody of him."

Kate threw her head back and laughed.

"Well, I have no intentions of filing any time soon," she assured him. Then, she wrapped her arms around Michael's neck and pressed her forehead to his. "I love you." Oh, it felt so good to finally be able to say that to a living, breathing boyfriend and not to a computer screen.

"I love you, too," Michael whispered back. Then after a pause, he added, "That did it."

"Did what?"

"We're alone. *Really* alone."

The way he looked at her, the way he softened his voice, sent shivers all the way down Kate's spine. How had she existed without him for the past six weeks? How had she existed without him at all?

Then he was kissing her and she was kissing him back, pressing her body against his in a desperate attempt to make up for all the time they'd spent apart. She felt his hands cupping her face, his long, slender fingers gripping her hair. For a fleeting instant, she could swear she felt his heart beating as she ran her lips along his jawline and down his neck.

"Come with me," she whispered. And then, dizzy and light-headed with love and desire, Kate took both of his hands and pulled him gently into his bedroom.

Lying in bed next to Kate, Michael found himself struggling to form a coherent thought.

Passion.

Ecstasy.

Golden.

Heaven.

Love.

A rapturous array of emotions and images and words flooded Michael's body, mind, and spirit as Kate smiled down at him, her shimmering sunlit hair cascading over her shoulders and brushing against his bare chest.

Marry me, a small voice in the back of his mind whispered over and over again. *Marry me. Marry me.*

In his state of intoxicated bliss, Michael seriously considered asking Kate right then, right there. He had the ring. He'd unpacked it and stashed it away in his sock drawer before she arrived. A few strides across the bedroom and he'd have it. It was so easy, so tempting....

And yet, something inside held him back. He wanted to propose to Kate more than anything. He needed her, the very way he needed air to breathe. But he also wanted their engagement to be special, something extraordinary. Nothing too grand, of course. He knew Kate didn't need the typical all-American proposal, sipping sparkling champagne in a five-star restaurant while a crowd of faceless onlookers politely applauded. No, it needed to be something heartfelt, something personal, something that would sweep Kate right off her feet.

"What are you thinking about?" she asked, her hazel eyes alight with love and just a hint of mischief.

"How I'm never leaving you again." The answer came naturally to him.

"Good." Kate tucked a lock of hair behind her ear, leaned down, and kissed him. It was a slow, tender kiss, and once again, Michael's thoughts drifted back to the diamond ring in his dresser.

Breaking away, he wrapped his arms around her and pulled her down into a tight embrace.

"God, I love you," he murmured into her hair. He'd spoken the words at least half a dozen times in the past hour, but he couldn't stop them from escaping his lips once more.

Unfortunately, he couldn't stop a low, rumbling growl from escaping his stomach, either. His long day of travel and poor diet of Dr. Pepper and airplane peanuts had left him famished. Kate, of course, threw her head back and laughed.

"I think that's my cue to go make dinner," she teased.

"You know, you don't *have* to make anything. We could always order in. That way you wouldn't have to do any work." *Or leave this bed*, Michael added mentally.

"I don't mind. I want to. I was talking to Gavin about what I could do for you when you came home and he suggested a good, home-cooked meal. Apparently, to you guys, food equals love."

"Will you at least let me help?" he asked.

14

"I'll let you pour the wine and light the candles. Maybe mince a few garlic cloves. I'd also be willing to let you do the dishes when we're done." Now it was Michael's turn to laugh.

"Wait a minute. I thought this was your welcome home gift to me."

"You asked if you could help!"

"I've been on a plane all day!"

"I've been here without you for six weeks."

Michael sighed. She had him there.

"Okay, I'll do the dishes. Tomorrow."

Kate grinned and kissed him on the cheek.

"I'll stick around and help," she offered as she closed the space between them, wrapping her arms around his shoulders and kissing the crook of his neck. Then, far more abruptly than Michael would have preferred, Kate leapt up out of bed and said, "But for now, I'm going to go and preheat the oven."

After she disappeared, Michael lingered a moment longer, casting one last contemplative glance toward his dresser.

No. She deserves more than an impromptu proposal in your apartment. Be patient. Wait for the moment.

Casting temptation out of his mind, he pulled his shirt back over his head and prepared to join Kate in the kitchen. But not before grabbing his phone and texting a quick message to Kate's father, asking if he might be free to talk any time in the coming week.

CHAPTER THREE

For as long as he could remember, all Michael had ever wanted was to be a normal guy. In his younger years, he would have traded anything and everything to not have to worry about anything more than changing the oil in his car or paying his taxes on time. That kind of life seemed like a dream come true compared to constantly having to dodge the ghosts of confused and angry dead people.

But now that he was about to ask a man for permission to marry his daughter, suddenly those restless spirits didn't seem all that daunting.

Mr. Avery must have had at least a bit of an inkling as to why Michael had asked to speak with him in private because he invited him over for drinks, conveniently, when Mrs. Avery was scheduled to be out with friends. Michael could at least breathe a little easier knowing that he would be able to talk with Rex without being subjected to Terri's disapproving glare.

When he finally arrived at the Avery house, Michael made the short walk from the driveway up the steps to the front porch, took a deep breath, and knocked on the door. While he waited, he wiped his clammy hands off on his jeans and prayed to whatever deity was out there that he wouldn't throw up before he got the words out.

Although Rex answered the door only moments later, Michael felt he had just spent an eternity on that front porch.

"Michael. Good to see you, son," Rex greeted him with a smile and a sturdy handshake.

"Good to see you too, Mr. Avery. Thank you for having me."

"Kid, how many times do I have to tell you to call me Rex?"

"Sorry, Sir."

Although he wasn't nearly as frightening as Terri with her overprotective-mom persona, Rex was, at the very least, a little intimidating. He was a typical guy's guy, large in stature and sports-centric in nature. He could probably snap Michael like a twig if he really wanted to. Michael kept that in mind as he followed Rex into Kate's childhood home. It was a very warm house, comfortable and cozy, with decades-old furniture, antique books, and dozens of gold-framed photographs of Kate and Gavin as kids lining the shelves.

"Can I offer you a beer?" Rex asked.

"Um, no thank you." Michael had never really been the drinking-before-five type. Or the drinking-anything-ever type. Not that he had any sort of opposition to it. He simply never knew how alcohol may affect him. It would more than likely loosen his inhibitions which, knowing his luck, would probably open him up to even more ghosts and weird spiritual energy and God knew what else.

"Soda then?" Rex asked.

"That would be great. Thank you."

Rex disappeared into the kitchen and returned, moments later, with a cold can of Dr. Pepper.

"Cheers," Rex said, popping open his own can of beer and taking a seat on the couch. Michael followed suit. "Now then. What can I do for you?"

For a split second, Michael didn't think he'd be able to go through with it. How did this work? Was he supposed to just come out and say it? *"Mr. Avery, I want to marry your daughter."* Or should there be at least a little bit of build up? Maybe an impassioned speech about how much he loved Kate and a list of reasons why he was the right man for her. God, he hoped he was good enough for her.

"Mr. Avery. I - " His voice cracked. Great. He drew in a shaky breath and tried again. "I wanted to talk to you... about..."

Come on, come on. Please don't be a coward. Not now. Not in front of him.

"Michael." Rex rested a large hand on Michael's shoulder. "Is this about Kate?"

"Yes, Sir," he answered sheepishly. Rex already knew why he was there. Of course he did. He was a smart man. And Michael was an idiot. Why couldn't he be confident like Brink or Luke? Neither of them would have worked themselves up into a panic attack over a simple question.

"It's okay, son. Breathe. You can do this," Rex assured him.

The older man's faith in him was comforting and slowly but surely, Michael began to relax.

"Mr. Avery, I love Kate more than anything in the world. I - I don't think I truly understood what it meant to really love someone until I met her, and I want nothing more than to love her and cherish her for the rest of our lives. What I'm saying, Sir..." Michael closed his eyes. His heart was beginning to race again. *You can do this. You can do this.* "Please, may I have your permission to ask her to marry me?"

Rex chuckled and took a swig of beer. Michael couldn't be certain, but for some reason, he got the feeling that Rex was proud of him.

"You know, I don't think there are too many fathers out there who can say something like this, but Michael, I knew you were the one for her the first time she ever talked about you."

"You did?"

"I really did," Rex told him. "She just had this look in her eye. This sparkle. I've seen her in love before. She was crazy about Trevor, loved him with all her heart. But even then, I didn't see *that* look until she met you."

Michael didn't know how to respond to that. He'd gone into his relationship with Kate knowing that he could never replace Trevor, nor did he ever intend to. He knew she still valued the love they'd had for one another and he knew that, in a way, she still mourned for him. But he also couldn't deny the burst of joy that he felt upon hearing her father's confession.

"Thank you," Michael said.

"You're welcome. Now, I hope you don't take this the wrong way, but you are white as a sheet. Are you okay?"

"Oh, yeah. I'm fine," Michael lied.

"I'd have thought with you out there fighting all those spooks, something like this would be a piece of cake for you." Now, Rex was laughing.

"Frankly, Sir, I am far less terrified of the spooks," Michael admitted with a wry grin.

"Well, you don't have to be," Rex told him. "You're already family. As far as I'm concerned, you've been family ever since you saved Kate's life last summer. And again, last October." Michael must have looked as stunned as he felt because Rex explained, "Don't worry, Terri doesn't know what happened. But Kate told me one night when it was just the two of us. In fact, it must have been around the time your book came out because it began with her telling me all about the process and how hard you've worked. Oh, you should have heard her. She is so proud of you. You're her hero. Well, besides her old man, of course."

"Thank you, Rex. Truly," Michael said.

"You're a good man, Michael. I know you'll take care of my little girl. You already do."

"I will. I promise."

"Then, go with my blessing. Although, if I may offer just one piece of advice?"

"Of course," Michael answered.

"Before you pop the question, take a shot of whiskey. It'll do you a world of good. Trust me, you don't want to be tripping over your words when you're asking the woman of your dreams to become your wife."

It wasn't exactly the counsel that Michael had been expecting, but he appreciated it nevertheless. Not because it was particularly sound advice or that he planned on taking it, but because it was very much advice that a father might give to a son. Michael had never known what it was like to have a father, or if he did, those memories of before his own father left were few and far between. In all those years, he'd never once wished for his father to return, because in a way, he felt like that would be a betrayal to his mother, who'd worked night and day to see that neither he nor his brother ever wanted for anything. But if his dad had been a man like Rex, who loved and protected and honored his family, Michael couldn't help but think it would have been nice to have him around.

"I'll keep that in mind," Michael smiled, hoping he didn't sound overly sentimental.

"I wish you the best of luck, kid. I truly do. But you're not gonna need it. Like I said, Kate has been in love with you from the very beginning."

Michael blushed.

"That makes two of us."

As he drove home, Michael thought of nothing but when and where he could propose to Kate.

Sunset picnic?
Too many mosquitos.
Family lake house?
Too much pressure.
Fancy dinner?
Too cliché.
Haunted cemetery?
Yeah, right.

He was so preoccupied that he didn't even register the news camera waiting for him outside of his apartment until a bold and energetic young woman was thrusting a microphone in his face.

"Mr. Sinclair! There you are! Tricia Montgomery, *TMZ*. Do you mind if I ask you a few questions?"

"Uh... I'm sorry... What's going on?" Surely *TMZ* had more interesting things to report on than his book release. There had to be some sort of scandal brewing in the darkest depths of Hollywood. An affair. A break-up. Or maybe even a happier occurrence like a wedding or an engagement or...

Wait a minute.

No. There was no way. How could *TMZ* possibly have found out? Besides Rex, the only person who knew he was planning to pop the question was a dead eighteen-year-old skater kid who still thought that wearing a long-sleeved flannel shirt tied around the waist was "totally rad." Even if he had figured out a way to talk to someone, no one alive would actually take him seriously.

"We promise not to take up too much of your time. We just wanted to know if and how you were planning to respond to Caleb Hayes' accusations."

"Who?"

"Michael!"

And like an angel sent from above, Kate raced down the stairs, grabbed him by the elbow, and pulled him away from Tricia Montgomery and her intrusive microphone.

"Miss Avery! Do you have any comments?" Tricia called after her.

"No, but thanks for stopping by!" Kate hollered from the second-story platform that separated her front door from Michael's. Then, she dragged Michael into her apartment and locked the door behind them. "Have you checked your social media recently?" she finally asked him.

"No..." Despite Luke's insistence that Twitter and Facebook were a great way to connect with readers, Michael rarely signed in to his accounts.

Kate reached into her pocket and pulled out her phone.

"Read this," she told him, holding the screen up for him to see.

"Michael Sinclair: The Supernatural Charlatan?" Uh-oh. That couldn't be good. *"The idea that the human spirit lives on after death is not a new one. In fact, supposed encounters with the dearly departed date all the way back to 930 BCE. That's nearly three thousand years of superstition, of senseless ritual, and of human deception. Generation after generation, self-proclaimed psychics, mediums, and ghost-hunters have preyed on the emotions and the vulnerability of the grieving and the bereaved.*

"Michael Sinclair is only one such individual, but he is the one that raises the most cause for concern. For you see, unlike his fellow "psychics," Michael Sinclair does not sing his own praises in the streets or shout his successes from the rooftops. He takes a far more devious approach. He presents himself as a victim, a sympathetic character."

"It goes on like that for a while," Kate warned him.

"Who is this guy?" Michael asked.

"Dr. Caleb Hayes. He's a professor of psychiatry out in Oregon. Luke's mentioned him once or twice. He calls him an outspoken skeptic."

"So Luke knows him?"

"He knows *of* him. As far as I know, they've never met. But Hayes has called him out in the past, kind of like he's doing to you."

"I bet Luke took that *really* well," Michael remarked.

"Surprisingly, their feud never escalated beyond a few passive-aggressive tweets. But that might change once Luke gets his hands on that article."

"Why?"

"Check out the last few paragraphs."

Michael did as she said.

"Here are the facts, plain and simple: ghosts do not exist. And if they did, I doubt they'd want to waste one second of their eternity performing circus tricks for the likes of Luke Rainer or seeking out an individual as unstable as Michael Sinclair for a posthumous therapy session. These truths, however, will not discourage tens of thousands from believing that these two men actually make contact with the spirits of the dead and that they do so on a regular basis.

"I understand why they want to believe. I do. After all, if life doesn't end with death, then there's no reason to fear death. Those who've suffered a loss no longer have to wonder if they will one day be reunited with their loved one. Not when they have Michael Sinclair assuring them that he just had pizza with their dead relative and hey, they're doing great. Don't worry.

"I do worry, though. I worry for those who will live out their lives with a devastating and quite possibly debilitating sense of false hope. I worry for the willfully ignorant. The ones who allow themselves to be deceived by men like Sinclair and Rainer. The ones who will argue against all logic and reason. The ones who prefer fiction to facts, solely for the sake of their own comfort. And Michael Sinclair and Luke Rainer are enabling and crippling each and every one of them.

"It's high time that we, as a society, stopped believing in fairy tales. We have one life. That life is here and now. If we're to make the best of our finite time, we must resist dwelling on what we hope to be true and instead, concentrate on what we know to be true."

Michael didn't know what to think, or what to say. Sure, there were book reviewers who'd dragged him through the mud and then back again, but somehow, none of those reviews ever felt like a personal attack. This article, on the other hand, had been written with passion. Passionate disapproval. Passionate disdain. By a man Michael had never even heard of.

"Are you okay?" Kate asked.

"I don't know," Michael answered. "How many people do you think have read this?"

23

It was a stupid question. Clearly the article had spread to more than just a few psychiatry enthusiasts. Otherwise, TMZ wouldn't have set up camp fifteen feet below his bedroom window.

"Hayes published it this morning. It went viral about three hours later."

"So, it's everywhere."

"Pretty much."

"Perfect." Michael fell backward onto Kate's couch and ran a hand through his already messy hair. Kate took a seat next to him and wrapped a loving and reassuring arm around his waist. Then she kissed him on the cheek. And then on the lips. Finally, Michael looked at her. "What would you do?"

"Well first, I'd probably cry," she admitted. Michael knew she was trying to lighten the mood, and he loved her for it. "To be honest, though, I think I'd just ignore him. If he's written this hoping to pick a fight with you, then lashing out at him would just be giving him what he wants. And if he isn't trying to start something, he's probably still expecting you to at least defend yourself."

"And you don't think I should?"

"Personally, I wouldn't waste the energy. Quarreling with anyone is exhausting. And quarreling with strangers online can be even worse because you have no idea who you're going up against."

"Well, in this case, it's a guy with an off-the-charts IQ and a doctorate to prove it."

"Yeah, and an ego to match it. Which is another reason I advise just letting it go. You can't win with guys like him. They won't let you," Kate told him. "I know it's easier said than done, but I really think that the best thing to do would be to just forget about Caleb Hayes. Chances are within a few, the rest of the world will have forgotten about him too."

CHAPTER FOUR

"Who's ignorant now, you crazy elitist bastard? Take that! HA!" Luke exclaimed as he sent yet another triumphant tweet spiraling into cyberspace.

"I thought you weren't going to fight with that guy anymore," his friend, J.T. Sawyer remarked.

"And I thought you weren't going to slurp your Ramen anymore, but life is full of fun little lies." Luke glared at his costar and, for the night, hotel roommate as the latter took a long swig from his near-empty bowl of noodles.

"I can't help it. It's so delicious."

"And Caleb Hayes is a steaming pile of pretentious pig manure," Luke seethed.

"Thanks for that lovely visual. I'm really glad I decided to go with the pork belly Ramen tonight."

"You know, he's written crap like this before, but this is different. This is a challenge. And I'm tired of taking it lying down."

"Lying down? You've never taken it lying down. You always fight back, which is why this guy keeps going after you. He knows he can rattle your chains and every time you snap back at him, you add fuel to the fire."

"Yeah, but it's not just me anymore. I know that Mikey is all grown up and can look after himself now, but I still feel responsible for him. He's like a little brother. Or a Tamagotchi."

"You were a terrible Tamagotchi parent."

"The point is that even though he's made a lot of progress, Mikey is still a very sensitive guy. Something like this could easily send him right back into his bubble of isolation and self-denial. And I'm sorry, but I've worked too hard to let that happen."

"Has he said anything to you? Or posted anything online?"

"No, but he's not really an internet guy. I think the last time he logged into Twitter was to retweet something Kate posted about his book. And that was almost two months ago."

"If that's the case, then maybe he doesn't know."

"Maybe, but unlike Mikey, Kate is a social media savant. If it's posted, she knows about it. And if she knows about it, he knows about it." Then, as if on cue, Luke's phone began to ring. Kate's name and three bird emojis lit up the screen. He answered with a satisfied smirk. "If I didn't already believe in psychic connections, this phone call would have me convinced."

"Oh, great. What does that mean?" It wasn't Kate who asked the question. It was Mikey. Luke realized that he must be on speakerphone.

"It means we're talking about you, Mikey!" Luke laughed.

"Who's we?"

"Me and J.T. We're roomies tonight. Say hi, J.T.!" J.T. mumbled something akin to a greeting through his last mouthful of Ramen. "He says hi."

"Hi, ghost hunters," Kate's cheerful voice echoed in Luke's ear. "So I'm guessing you're not actually investigating tonight since my phone chimes every other minute with a new notification from you."

"Aw. You get my Twitter alerts? That's sweet," Luke smiled.

"It would be sweeter if you'd stop trying to provoke the guy who just wrote a scathing article blasting my boyfriend."

"I'm not trying to provoke him. I'm trying to *educate* him."

"Is that what you call it? Because I've got to tell you, it's not often that you hear words like 'arrogant blowhard' in the classroom."

"Some lessons are hard to teach." And even harder to learn.

"Be that as it may, it might be a little easier on all of us if you'd, you know, quit while you were ahead."

"But he's wrong and he needs to know that," Luke explained.

"But what if this isn't the way to let him know? What if you're not doing yourself any favors? I understand that you're angry. We're angry, too. But there has to be a better way to resolve this, don't you think?"

She had a point. Luke didn't want to admit it. But she had a point. There probably was a better way to deal with Hayes, but unfortunately, for the moment, a Twitter handle was all that Luke had to work with. If only he didn't live halfway across the country.

"Well, you know, I'll actually be home for a couple of days next week. Maybe we can have dinner and try to come up with a plan of action," Luke said.

"I think we'd like that," Kate told him. "And who knows? Maybe by then, all of this will have died down. Maybe by then, we won't need a plan of action."

That would be nice, though it didn't seem likely. Until Caleb Hayes wrote an equally lengthy letter of apology, stating not only that he was wrong to criticize two such remarkable individuals as Luke and Mikey but that ghosts absolutely, positively, beyond a shadow of a doubt existed, nothing would be settled. Of course, that wasn't going to happen. Not without cold, concrete, indisputable evidence. And even that might not be enough to convince the Skeptic Extraordinaire.

It was too bad Hayes couldn't meet a ghost for himself.
... Or could he?

"You know what? That sounds great!" Luke suddenly exclaimed. "Hey listen, Lovely, something has just come up and I've got to go, but I'll text you about next week. Okay, bye!" He wasn't sure if what he said made any sense at all, but his mind was working a mile a minute. And as soon as he'd hung up on Kate, he was Googling Caleb Hayes' contact information.

It didn't take long to find a number. Hopefully, he was still at his office.

Sure enough, he picked up on the second ring.

"This is Dr. Hayes."

God, he even answered the phone like a pretentious snob.

"Hayes, how goes it? This is Luke Rainer."

"Luke *Rainer*?"

"The one and only. Listen, I've got a proposition for you..."

A week had passed since the Caleb Hayes debacle and Michael was feeling cautiously optimistic. He'd expected at least a minor fallout, perhaps a plunge in book sales or an onslaught of negative reviews. Maybe follow-up pieces from fans of Hayes or even Hayes himself. But aside from a few reporters reaching out for comments, it seemed that the article had had absolutely no impact at all.

Kate was right. It was as though Caleb Hayes had never existed.

That meant that Michael was finally free to concentrate on more important things. Planning the perfect proposal for example. Unfortunately, that was proving to be a task even trickier than editing and re-editing the same manuscript four times over.

He'd called his mother to ask her for advice and of course, she gave him the typical mom response.

"When and where won't matter to her, Michael. All that matters is that you love her."

She made it sound so simple! And maybe, in a way, that's how it was supposed to be. A simple moment, a simple gesture, a simple statement to say that he wanted to spend the rest of his life with her. But Kate deserved so much more than simple. And somehow, nothing Michael could come up with seemed good enough. Not as far as he was concerned, anyway.

That's why, when Luke texted to confirm their plans for dinner, Michael asked if he wanted to grab a drink, just the two of them, before they met up with Kate. Given Luke's history of slipshod secret-keeping, this was an admittedly questionable decision on Michael's part. Still, Luke was one of Kate's best friends. Maybe he'd have an idea.

They agreed to meet up at a local bar and grill an hour before Kate was scheduled to get off work. Luke was already there when Michael arrived, nursing a beer and staring at his phone while a baseball game played on the television in the background.

"Hey, Mikey!" Luke greeted his friend with a sunny grin. "Get this. There's a Pokémon Go stop right outside and someone just set a lure. I swear, the world loves me today."

"That's fantastic, Luke." Michael tried not to sound snarky, but sometimes, he couldn't help it. Thankfully, Luke didn't seem to notice.

"So, how's the author life?" he asked, setting his phone aside. "Enjoying your time off? Or are you diving right back into book two?"

"Honestly, I don't know that there's all that much more to write," Michael answered.

"Oh, sure there is. You just need to put yourself out there. Ed and Lorraine Warren wrote six books about their encounters with the paranormal."

Yeah, but they went looking for ghosts on purpose. Although Michael knew he'd made great strides toward accepting his admittedly creepy lot in life, he still wasn't to the point of embracing it with open arms.

"Didn't they also tackle demonic possessions?" Michael asked.

"Yeah, but you don't have to go that far. Unless you want to," Luke grinned.

"No, I think I'll pass on the demons."

"I wonder what *they'd* look like?" Luke pressed.

"I can't think of anything I'd rather not know," Michael countered.

"You never want to have any fun, do you?"

"Since when are demons fun?"

Luke didn't seem to have a real answer for that one, so he changed the subject.

"So, have you heard where we're headed next week?" he asked. Michael could only assume he meant the *Cemetery Tours* crew.

"No." Then again, Kate may have told him and he'd simply forgotten.

"Well, try not to be too jealous. Next Friday, the team and I are jetting off to Scotland, homeland of haggis, Nessie, and my great-grandfather, Arthur."

"Scotland, wow!" Michael hated to admit it, but he actually was jealous. "How long will you be there?"

"Eight days. We're going to be filming all over the country for our two-hour long Halloween special. We'll start in Edinburgh, make our way up to the Highlands, then ferry over to the Isle of Iona. Then we'll have a day or two in Stirling before flying out."

"That sounds incredible." Yeah, Michael was definitely jealous. Throughout his college years, he'd always dreamed of studying abroad, but he'd never been able to afford it. Scotland, with its castles and legends and misty mountains, seemed a land straight out of a fairy tale. It would be the perfect place for a honeymoon.

... Or a proposal.

"You haven't even heard the best part. I - "

"Can we go with you?" Michael honestly didn't mean to interrupt Luke, but the words were tumbling out of his mouth before he could stop them.

"What?" Luke raised his eyebrows, looking quite certain that he hadn't heard him correctly.

"Kate and me, that is," Michael clarified, well aware of how tactless he was being. But he didn't care. "Can we go to Scotland with you?"

"Are you kidding? Yeah! I mean, it's a little last minute, and we'll have to make sure we can get you on the same flight. Of course, you're going to need your passports. Oh, and you'll have to make sure that Kate can take the time off of work. And judging by the look on your face, you haven't thought any of this through at all. That's all right, that's all right. Anything is possible, especially if you know the right people. And I do. Besides, this is a once-in-a-lifetime opportunity! Speaking of which, would you want to be a guest on the show again? Because you've never volunteered for something like this before. In fact, I'm fairly certain that after Stanton Hall Manor, you swore off anything and everything having to do with paranormal investigating until the day you die and *you're* the one that the paranormal investigators are hoping to make contact with."

Michael wasn't about to even attempt to make sense of that.

"So... Is that a yes?" he asked.

"Hell yeah, I already told you! You and Kate are welcome to join the team any time. I'm just a little surprised that you *want* to come with us. That is, unless you're just looking for a free trip to Scotland, in which case, you're rich now. Use your own damn money."

"That's not it," Michael assured him. "The truth is I want to propose to Kate and I was thinking that - "

"Oh my God. Can I film it?" Luke blurted. "Sorry, that was rude. What I mean is congratulations on your eminent engagement! And, on that note, could I possibly have your permission to film and air said engagement on national television?"

Michael sighed.

"Why not?"

"Yes! Thank you!" Luke exclaimed. "In all seriousness, I am *really* happy for you. And for Kate. You guys are perfect for each other."

"Thanks, Luke."

"You're welcome. Now, just so she doesn't get suspicious, you should let me bring up Scotland. If you tell her that you've arranged for the two of you to go, it will look like you're planning something. Which you are. So, when she gets here, *I* will casually invite the two of you along. She will inevitably say yes. She's just got that adventurous spirit. Meanwhile, you will hesitate and act like your normal stick-in-the-mud self because, well, normally you would. But eventually, she will convince you to go as she always does and then you and I can work out all the boring stuff later. Sound like a plan?"

"Uh... Sure."

"Don't worry. I know that's a lot to remember. Just follow my lead and act natural. Like you're not planning a proposal."

"Good advice. Thanks."

"Eh. I do what I can," Luke shrugged.

When Kate arrived half an hour later, Luke greeted her by scooping her up in his arms and twirling her around.

"Good to see you, Gorgeous!" he exclaimed.

"You too, Luke! How long are you in town?"

"Just a few days. I actually have some pretty exciting news."

"Really?" Kate asked. "What is it?"

"I'll tell you in a minute. Let's get a table first," Luke answered, playing it cool.

Unlike most - for want of a better word - psychics, Michael had never been very in tune to the emotions or energies of those around him. Those living, anyway. But in that moment, he was so profoundly aware of the vibrant curiosity and eagerness radiating from Kate that Michael swore he could feel them himself.

Luke, meanwhile, was clearly enjoying watching her fidget while she waited for him to let her in on the big secret. Michael wondered for half a moment if he should act curious as well. Then he remembered that under normal circumstances, he probably wouldn't care. Or he'd be more than a little wary.

Finally, after they'd placed their orders, Kate burst.

"Okay, now tell us! What's the news?"

"Next week, the crew and I are going to begin production on our Halloween special... in Scotland!"

"Oh my God, I'm so jealous," Kate sighed. "I'd love to go to Scotland. Well, I mean, I've actually been to the UK once, but that was before... you know..."

Michael did know. Before the car accident that claimed more than two years of Kate's memories, including those of Trevor and her journey overseas. Although Kate had, for the most part, come to peace with the events of the past, she still didn't like to talk about them very much.

"Well, that's part of the reason I asked to meet you guys here," Luke lied smoothly. "Since this is such a special episode and Scotland is a dream come true to all of us, I was wondering if the two of you might want to come along."

Kate gasped.

"Are you serious?!" she squealed.

Michael grinned like an idiot until he remembered that this was supposed to be the first time he was hearing all this as well.

"Wow, Luke. Uh... I don't know what to say."

"Easy, Mikey. You say, 'Thanks, pal. We'd love to come,'" Luke winked.

"Oh my God. Oh my God. Is this possible?" Kate wondered. "I mean, can we go on such short notice? I think my passport is still good, but what about tickets? Will we be able to afford them? And where will we stay?"

"We've got you covered on the room and board thing. No worries," Luke winked.

"Michael, what do you think?" Kate exclaimed. "I know Val will give me the time off. At least, I'm pretty sure she will. It is a little last minute, but I think she'll understand. How long will we be gone?"

"We'll be there eight days. Allow two for travel," Luke answered. Then, he turned to Michael. "So, Mikey, are you in on this or what?"

Michael pretended to hesitate, just as Luke had advised. He'd have thought that years of acting like he didn't have a sixth sense might have left him with a few decent tricks of the trade, but he feared he was just as unconvincing as he'd been the first time he'd tried to deny his feelings for Kate.

"Gee, Luke, I don't know... Are you sure about this?"

"Mikey, when am I ever not sure about something?"

Oh, there was a question with a million answers. But Michael held his tongue. After all, Luke really had become one of his best friends. He was always willing and happy to help out, which was more than Michael could say for most people, even himself. Especially himself. It had taken him a few years, but he had finally come to realize just how lucky he was to have a friend like Luke, and it was time he stopped making fun of him and taking him for granted.

Michael cast one last glance at Kate, whose hopeful gaze hadn't left his face for even half a second. Then, he heaved as relenting a sigh as he could muster and tried not to smile.

"Okay. Let's go to Scotland."

CHAPTER FIVE

So Luke hadn't told them. So what? It really wasn't that big a deal. They were getting an incredibly affordable trip to Scotland, after all. And it was Mikey's idea that they come along in the first place. Luke wasn't about to crush his sappy, romantic hopes and dreams by mentioning that someone else would be meeting them at Edinburgh Airport.

Or, you know, that that someone happened to be Dr. Blowhard himself, Caleb Hayes.

He'd contemplated telling them when they showed up at DFW Airport earlier that morning, but Kate looked so excited and Mikey was actually trusting him for once and Luke just couldn't bear to break it to them. In a way, he was doing everyone a favor. He knew the moment that they found out, he was going to be in for one hell of a lecture. From whom, he wasn't quite sure. Usually, his money would have been on Mikey, but after Kate had called to chastise him for his admittedly aggressive tweets, he wouldn't be surprised if she had a few choice words of her own for him. Either way, that seven-hour flight over the Atlantic wouldn't be nearly as long as it would have been with one or both of them harboring any sort of animosity towards him.

So, he just decided to conveniently forget the whole thing and focus, instead, on the journey ahead. And of course, that meant keeping all of his fans up-to-date on the goings-on of their favorite paranormal investigators.

With a smile, he opened the Instagram app on his phone and began to live-stream.

"Hey, guys! We're here at our layover in New Jersey. Still have a few hours before our plane leaves so we're cruising the gift shops, checking out the food court, and trying to keep Mikey's enthusiasm in check." He panned the video over to Mikey, who looked remarkably unimpressed for a guy who was about to get engaged to his gorgeous girlfriend in Scotland. "Smile, Mikey! You're on Instagram!"

Mikey didn't smile.

"He's still not crazy about social media," Kate explained. "It took him forever to finally confirm that we were in a relationship on Facebook."

"Well, get over your aversion, my friend. I am documenting this entire trip. I mean, you knew I was going to be documenting because we're filming. But thanks to the beauty of the live-stream, I can show everyone what goes on behind the scenes. All. The. Time."

"You'll learn to tune him out eventually," J.T. assured Mikey as the live-stream came to an end.

It was at that point in the conversation that Luke expected Mikey to make some snide remark about having learned to tune Luke out a long time ago, but shockingly enough, he held his tongue. Maybe he was secretly in a good mood after all and just really playing it up for Kate and the cameras.

"So, Kate, I've been meaning to ask you... How's Gavin doing?" Gail Marsh, another of Luke's costars, wanted to know. Luke shot her a look as J.T. visibly tensed. "What? It's an innocent question."

"He's great," Kate answered. "He's got a job with a film company that he really loves. He's saving up for a new car. You know, life is good."

"Is he uh... seeing anyone?"

"Gail," Luke warned.

"What?! We're not working yet! And he's not even here!"

"I don't care. It's still inappropriate."

"*How*?!"

"Guys, guys, come on," Peter Jamison, the fourth member of the *Cemetery Tours* crew and perpetual peacemaker, intervened. "This is going to be the coolest experience of our lives. Are we really going to get into this *right now*?"

"He started it," Gail muttered.

Luke glared at her, but before he could say anything, Mikey asked, "Hey Luke, how's Claire?" in a blatant attempt to change the subject and ease the tension.

"She's great, Mikey, thanks for asking."

"Oh, right. Luke's ghost girlfriend," Gail rolled her eyes.

"She's not my girlfriend," Luke repeated for the thousandth time. "She's my research partner. With her help, I've been able to record some fascinating electronic voice phenomena and I've managed to capture her shadow on video. However, we're still struggling a bit with the photography. But she likes having a purpose, and she's told me a lot of amazing stories."

"If you love her so much, then why isn't she invited on any of these investigations?" Gail asked.

"Because when we're invited to a new location, we are there to observe and validate and interact with those spirits. Claire understands. Besides, she probably enjoys getting a break from me once in a while."

"Who wouldn't?" Gail muttered.

Luke ignored her.

"Okay, since we're all together, I want to go ahead and let you know what the plan is for the next thirty-six hours or so," he said. "J.T., Gail, Peter, you've done overseas trips before, so you pretty much know the drill. But Mikey and Kate, you guys should know that once we land in Scotland tomorrow morning, we are hitting the ground running. They're five hours ahead of us, six if you're still on Texas time. That means we have to beat the jet lag. If at all possible, try to get as much sleep on the plane as you can because you won't be sleeping again for a while. Any questions?"

"I have one. Where are you actually going to be investigating?" Kate asked.

"That is a very good question, Beautiful. Since this is our Halloween special, we're actually dividing our time between two different locations. The first is the city of Edinburgh. Our first night there, we'll be investigating Greyfriars Kirkyard, Edinburgh Castle, and the Edinburgh Vaults. Then we'll journey north to investigate the ghosts of the Highlands. We'll actually be staying several nights in Dunadhar Castle but one night, we're going to be camping out at Loch Ness, just to see if we can catch a glimpse of Nessie."

"Branching out, huh?" Mikey asked.

"Don't tell me you're not a believer, Mikey."

"In a massive sea dragon?"

Luke sighed.

Everyone's a skeptic.

Kate tried to take Luke's advice and get some sleep on the plane, but hour after hour, her mind continued to race with nervous energy and worst-case-disaster scenarios. Flying had never been her favorite way to get around. Every time they hit even the slightest bit of turbulence, Kate imagined the plane plummeting from the sky and into the dark, vast, fathomless ocean below.

Don't worry. You're okay. You've made this flight before, remember?

That's the problem, she argued against her own mind. *I don't remember.*

She knew she'd crossed the Atlantic when she'd traveled to London with Trevor, and while that should have comforted her, the fact of the matter was it left her anxiety-riddled brain reeling with unanswered questions and echoes of moments that may as well have never happened.

Squeezing her eyes shut, she forced herself to concentrate on Michael. On his scent, on his warmth, on the sound of his soft, even breathing. Any other night and his presence alone would have been enough to soothe her to sleep. Tonight, however, she was wide awake.

Almost as though he sensed her discomfort, Michael stirred, shifted in his seat, and gazed at her with sleepy eyes.

"Are you all right?" he whispered.

"I will be," she assured him, lacing her fingers deftly through his. "Go back to sleep." Michael closed his eyes, but moments later, he chuckled and opened them again. "What?"

"Brink says that if you could hear him, he'd sing you a lullaby."

At that, Kate actually smiled.

"That's sweet."

"Trust me, you're not missing out," Michael teased.

"It's the thought that counts."

"Now he says he wishes you *were* the one who could hear him because I don't know how to appreciate him the way that you do. And you're prettier than me."

"I don't think that's fair. You're beautiful," Kate smiled, resting her head against Michael's shoulder.

"Now Brink's laughing at me," he murmured, pressing his lips against her forehead.

"He's just jealous," Kate yawned.

Finally, *finally*, she was beginning to relax. She closed her eyes and let her mind wander to far-off lands, to fairy-tale castles and majestic mountains. She imagined waking to the sound of bagpipes and walking the historic pathways of warriors and saints and kings. And in that last moment, before she drifted off to sleep, she saw Michael, handsome and radiant against the backdrop of the setting Scottish sun while the waters of Loch Ness danced in the distance.

Not once did she spare a thought for the ageless cemeteries, the haunting myths, or the lost souls that also waited for them.

She woke a mere few hours later to morning light streaking across the sky outside the airplane window. Michael still slept peacefully beside her, his dark hair falling adorably into his eyes. Across the aisle, however, Luke was already wide awake and snacking on a croissant and fruit.

"Good morning, Sunshine! Sleep well?"

"Slept okay."

"You want some breakfast? This melon is disgusting." He held out his fruit cup.

"So you're offering it to me?"

"I'm a gentleman."

"Yes, well, as much as I appreciate your generosity, I think I've got a granola bar stashed away in my backpack."

It was only as she leaned forward to grab her bag that she took another brief glance out the window. The clouds were beginning to part, revealing not a raging ocean, but soft, peaceful ground the color of the brightest emerald. Kate gasped and grabbed Michael's shoulder, startling him awake.

"Wha - ?" he asked, still half-asleep.

"Look!" Kate exclaimed. "Oh my God! It's breathtaking!"

"If you think it's beautiful now, just wait until we land," Luke grinned.

"Are we there yet?" Michael mumbled.

"Almost. If the plane's on time, we should be landing in a little over half an hour," Luke answered. "And that means..." He trailed off as he whipped out his phone and began to live-stream.

"Oh boy," Michael groaned.

"Good morning!" Luke greeted his cyber-fans. "And oh, what a beautiful morning it is! I have got to tell you, I am so stoked for this investigation. It is going to be unlike anything we've ever done before."

"You say that every time," J.T. commented from the window seat next to Luke.

"And I mean it every time. No investigation is like the one before it. And that is because every haunting is unique, just like every spirit is unique. But *this* is our going to be our most ambitious investigation, one that is guaranteed to leave a lasting impact not only on us, but on everyone who watches it. Stay tuned!"

Then Luke winked at the phone and shoved it back into his pocket.

"He's going to be doing this the entire trip," Michael hissed in Kate's ear.

"Be nice," Kate chided gently. Then, kissing him swiftly on the cheek, she added, "Remember, we're about to be in Scotland!"

And exactly thirty-two minutes later, they were.

Luke was right, Kate thought to herself, gazing out the window as the plane slowed to a stop. Scotland was *so* much more beautiful up close. Lush fields danced with mist just beyond the runways of Edinburgh Airport and although heavy clouds obscured the sun, Kate was certain that she had never seen a more glorious day.

Once they disembarked and made it through Customs, Kate caught herself once again daydreaming about everything they were about to experience. She couldn't wait to get out into the streets. She couldn't wait to play the tourist and take pictures in front of the Elephant House. And she really couldn't wait to get something to eat other than a granola bar and airplane cantaloupe.

"Do you dare me to try haggis?" Kate asked Michael as they all stood around, waiting to collect their luggage.

"That depends. Do you want to try haggis?"

"A little bit, yeah."

"Then yes. I dare you to try haggis," Michael grinned. That grin quickly faded, however, as he glanced over to his right. "No."

"What now, Brink?"

"No," Michael repeated to his invisible friend. Then, he sighed and turned his attention back to Kate. "Please tell him that it doesn't matter how much he wants to know what haggis tastes like, he's not allowed to possess you or anyone else while they're eating." At that, Kate threw her head back and laughed. "No! Don't encourage him!" Michael exclaimed.

"You know, Luke probably wouldn't say no..."

"Okay, this conversation ends now," Michael said. Then he added, "Yeah, well, you'd better get used to it."

"Better get used to what?"

"He says that the older we get, the more we act like his parents."

"Well, we do only want what's best for him."

"He believes that *you* want what's best for him. Somehow, he's convinced that I'm just here to ruin his life. Or his afterlife. Whatever."

"Nah, he knows you love him."

"Love is such a strong word..."

Kate snickered again as her bright, sunshine-colored suitcase finally made its way around the baggage carousel.

As soon as the entire crew had their bags, cameras, and cases in hand, they began their eager trudge out to the car park where, Luke had assured them, their bus driver was already waiting to help them load their luggage.

"His name is Bill. He's a really great guy. I met him a few years ago when I brought my mom here for her birthday. Trust me, you're going to love him," Luke insisted.

But the man waiting for them outside of the airport didn't seem the friendly sort. In fact, there was nothing warm or welcoming about him at all. Tall and rigid, with a sort of twisted air of authority about him, he watched them approach with eyes far too hardened for someone so young.

"I was beginning to think you'd set me up," the man addressed Luke without shaking his hand.

"Do you really think I'd do a thing like that?"

"I wouldn't put it past you."

"You don't even know me."

"I know enough," the man remarked lightly.

"I'm sorry. Who are you?" Kate asked.

"Ah, so Rainer didn't mention that I'd be joining you." His voice dripped with smug satisfaction, like he'd just won some sort of game only he knew that they were playing.

"No. He didn't," Michael stepped in, glaring at Luke.

"Michael Sinclair. Thought one of your ghost friends might have told you. But I guess even they don't know everything." The stranger was smiling now, but that smile didn't reach his beady, bespectacled eyes. "I'm Dr. Caleb Hayes. And I'm here to expose you once and for all."

CHAPTER SIX

Michael was too stunned to speak.

This was a mistake. It had to be some horrible, horrible mistake. The man staring him down couldn't possibly be Caleb Hayes. Caleb Hayes had no business being in Scotland. He was supposed to be back in Oregon writing destructive think-pieces and ruining hard-earned reputations. And even if the slightest chance existed that his presence there *could* be rationalized, nothing on God's green Earth explained Luke's lack of surprise to see him there.

But before Michael could convert his convoluted thoughts into reasonable words, Kate whirled around and confronted Luke with a sort of seething fury he'd never seen in her before.

"What the hell is this?" she demanded. "You *knew* he was going to be here?!"

"Well, uh... Yeah, kinda," Luke admitted.

"And you didn't think to mention it even *once*?!"

"I thought that if you knew, you might not want to come," Luke explained.

"So instead, you fly us halfway around the world without even a *hint* that the man who's out to make Michael's life a living hell would be waiting for us when we got there? How could you do that to us, Luke? I thought we were your friends."

"You are. That's why I wanted you here."

"Under false pretenses!"

"She's not wrong," Hayes remarked.

"Oh, shut up," Kate snapped at him.

"Kate, Lovely, please. I know you're pissed. And you have every reason to be. But just hear me out," Luke begged.

44

"Fine." Kate crossed her arms over her chest, raised a single brow, and stared at Luke with eyes that chilled Michael to the bone. He prayed to whatever deity happened to be listening that he never gave Kate a reason to turn those eyes on him.

"Believe it or not, I didn't invite him out of malice. It's like I told you the other night. As a paranormal researcher, I am called not only to investigate but to *educate* - "

"Oh, please." Hayes scoffed.

"Hey, I am trying to be civil here," Luke rebuked before turning back to Kate. "Anyway, when you called to chastise me, you astutely pointed out that there had to be a better way to resolve our differences than exchanging insults over Twitter. And you were right. So I called up Dr. Hayes here, who, if I may say so, turned out to be *just* as charming in person, though not quite what I was expecting - "

"I thought you were trying to be civil," Hayes remarked.

"And I thought you were some crotchety attic-dweller with a scraggly white beard and monocle. Are you even old enough to have a doctorate?"

"Luke!" Kate scolded.

"What? It's a compliment. Sort of."

Whether intended as a compliment or not, Michael had to admit that Luke did have a point. Caleb Hayes was much younger than he'd envisioned. Younger and trendier. He didn't bear the distinguished look of a stereotypical college professor. Instead, he wore torn and tattered jeans, a t-shirt bearing the name and logo of a Pacific coast brewery, and black-rimmed hipster glasses. His hair was just a shade lighter than Michael's, but he'd styled it much shorter and he appeared to be in the early stages of growing a beard.

"So uh... how old *are* you?" Gail asked Hayes.

"I'm thirty-four. Quite old enough to have a doctorate."

"Hmm. Old enough for a doctorate yet young enough to - "

"Gail, I *forbid* you to finish that sentence," Luke declared.

Gail just giggled. Hayes, much to Michael's surprise, smirked. He may not have believed in ghosts, but he definitely didn't seem to mind being flirted with by one of the world's favorite ghost hunters.

Almost as though he sensed Michael's silent accusation, Hayes turned and looked him up and down with cool, calculating eyes.

"We haven't heard much from you, Sinclair," he observed. "I have to admit, I'm disappointed."

"I'm sorry. What exactly were you hoping to hear?" Michael wondered.

"Frankly, I was anticipating a little animosity. I thought you'd at least attempt to challenge me on my article. But you don't put up much of a fight, do you?"

"I guess I just figured you weren't really worth my time." Michael didn't realize just how harsh the words sounded until they were out of his mouth. Of course, they didn't faze Hayes at all. If anything, he looked a little impressed, which was somehow even more annoying than his superior, condescending jerk charade.

Before Hayes could actually respond, however, a small bus pulled up to the curb. The doors opened and a short, middle-aged man with curly blond hair emerged and greeted Luke with a broad, toothy grin.

"Mr. Rainer! It's good to see you again!" he exclaimed with a thick Scottish accent.

"It's better to see you, Bill!" Luke replied. "Everyone, I'd like to introduce you to Bill McLaughlin, hands down the most amazing fellow you will ever meet."

"Ah, you're too kind," Bill smiled, brushing off Luke's praise with a modest wave of his hand.

"Not at all. I work only with the best and you, Sir, are the best. Now," Luke turned his attention back to his motley entourage. "What do you say we get this show on the road?"

"I'm ready!" Peter proclaimed with his usual enthusiasm.

"Okay, but just so you know, our conversation isn't over," Kate warned Luke as they began to gather their belongings.

"Oh Darling, I'd be a fool to think it was," Luke muttered.

The journey into the heart of Edinburgh was a relatively short one, only about thirty minutes or so, but it was more than enough time for Michael to reevaluate every hope he'd had for their trip. There was no way he could propose to Kate now, not with Hayes around. The possibility existed that he and Kate could simply extricate themselves from the group and spend the next week traveling the country just with each other. Unfortunately, that would also mean leaving Luke alone with Hayes, and Michael knew exactly how the latter would interpret his sudden disappearance. It would look like an admission of defeat, a confirmation that Hayes was right and that Michael was afraid to face him.

Michael had never considered himself a particularly proud person, but there was no way he was going to let that happen.

"Oh, my God! Look! Look!" Kate exclaimed, mercifully freeing Michael from his own brooding mind. He followed her gaze out the window to a magnificent castle perched atop a lofty hill.

"That's Edinburgh Castle, arguably one of the most haunted castles in Scotland," Luke said. "The first time I visited, they let me conduct an impromptu EVP session and I captured the voice of a little kid. I thought that was odd at first. But then our tour guide told us the story of the lost piper boy who disappeared in the secret underground tunnels connecting the castle to Holyroodhouse Palace. Now, centuries later, his ghost is said to still walk the Royal Mile."

"You really will believe anything you want to believe, won't you?" Hayes remarked.

"Hey, I can't help but believe what I know to be true," Luke responded.

"You mean what your eager mind tricks you into believing is true."

"Boy, this is going to be a fun week," Luke muttered as the bus came to a rolling stop in front of an elegant, three-story building with red doors and potted flowers on every balcony. "Okay, folks. This is our first stop."

"Sweet. What is this place? A Cathedral?" Peter asked.

"This is our hotel," Luke answered.

"Hey, that's pretty sweet too. Is it haunted?"

"We can always hope. Now then," Luke said, pausing to grab his backpack. "We've got about an hour before we're scheduled to take our walking tour of the Royal Mile. Take this opportunity if you will to settle in, shower, change, grab a bite to eat, because after the tour, we'll be spending the evening at Greyfriars Kirkyard. Any questions?"

"Yeah. What's a kirkyard?" J.T. asked.

"A churchyard. A church's graveyard. Any other questions?"

"Can we go to the Elephant House?" Gail asked.

"Well, duh," Luke answered.

"What's the Elephant House?" Michael whispered to Kate. She turned and looked at him with eyes that suddenly seemed to question everything she thought she knew about him. "What?"

"Just realizing that I've failed you not only as a girlfriend but as fangirl in general," she sighed.

"I don't know what that means."

"The Elephant House is the cafe where J.K. Rowling wrote the *Harry Potter* books," Kate explained. "In other words, it is hallowed ground."

"Ah," Michael said. He'd read and enjoyed the *Harry Potter* books, but he'd never been quite as spellbound by the boy wizard as Kate or Brink. Or the entire *Cemetery Tours* crew, apparently.

"All right, if there are no more questions, J.T., why don't you and Pete help the ladies unload their luggage. Hayes, I trust you can fend for yourself. Mikey, you come with me and we'll get checked in."

Michael agreed and followed Luke off the bus and into the hotel lobby. He was loath to leave Kate with the likes of Hayes, but he also knew that she was more than capable of fending for herself. Besides, she had the rest of the crew there with her. And he had a few choice words of his own for Luke that were not exactly suitable for polite company.

As usual, however, Luke spoke first.

"Okay, so before you say anything, let me just tell you that yes, I know I owe you the biggest apology ever. I'll be apologizing until one of us is dead and buried and the other is being haunted. Please believe me when I tell you that I'm sorry. I truly intended to say something when we met for lunch last week. But then you told me all about wanting to propose and you got so excited and then she got so excited that I just... I didn't want to ruin it for you."

"I don't know how to break it to you, Luke, but this is kind of worse."

"I know. I know, I know, and I am so sorry. But listen, I still think this could be a great trip. For you and for Kate."

"How, Luke? How could this possibly be a great trip? I can't propose to her now. She's feeling angry and betrayed and that's not how I want her to remember her engagement. Not to mention I'm going to have this Hayes guy breathing down my neck, analyzing my every move, just waiting for me to prove him right - "

"But you're not going to prove him right. You're going to prove him wrong which is the whole reason he's here."

"Come on. You really think a guy like that is ever going to admit that he's wrong about anything?"

"I got you to admit that you can see dead people, didn't I?" *Damn.* Luke was right. Michael hated it when Luke was right. But much to Michael's surprise, Luke didn't gloat about it or try to rub it in his face. In fact, his expression had actually softened. "Listen, I know how this looks. I know I was a lousy friend. But believe it or not, I didn't bring you or Kate out here to help me wage war on Caleb Hayes. I brought him here so that he could experience the paranormal first hand. So he could understand that thrill of knowing that life *is* more than what we know."

"Then why did you bring us?"

"Because you asked. Because I wanted to help you celebrate your success. And because I want you and Kate to have the happily ever after that you deserve. And you know, call me a hopeless romantic, but I'm daring to believe that you'll change your mind about being able to propose to her here."

"I appreciate that, Luke. But I really don't think that's going to happen."

Luke just shrugged.

"A lot can happen in a week, Mikey," he reminded him. "You should know that better than anyone."

CHAPTER SEVEN

Outside the gates of Holyroodhouse Palace, Luke, Gail, J.T., and Peter all worked diligently, readying themselves and their equipment so that they would be set to begin filming by the time their tour guide arrived. Kate and Mikey, meanwhile, wandered around hand-in-hand, whispering to each other and taking in the sights and sounds of their new setting. It relieved Luke to see them smiling and laughing together, although every once in a while, Kate would catch Luke's eye and throw him one of those I'm-not-angry-I'm-just-disappointed looks.

All things considered, Luke probably deserved it.

Hayes, meanwhile, was content to hover around the crew, watching with eyes like an irritatingly invasive hawk. Mikey may have had a point with that whole breathing-down-his-neck lecture.

But Gail didn't seem to mind Hayes' loitering at all.

"So, Caleb, are you ready for your *Cemetery Tours* debut?" she asked, flashing Hayes her brightest smile.

"I'm afraid I won't actually be appearing on the show," he told her.

"What? Why not?"

"It was one of our conditions," Hayes explained.

"Are you serious?" Gail demanded. "I can't believe you, Luke. Are you really so insecure that you told Caleb he wasn't allowed to be on the show?"

"Hey, for your information, that was *his* condition," Luke said.

"Really?" Gail asked, turning back to Hayes.

"When I accepted his offer, I made it very clear that my actions were not an endorsement and I didn't want them to be perceived as such, nor did I want him using my presence here as a gimmick on national television."

"Okay," J.T. spoke slowly, exchanging a wary glance with Luke. "Why did you agree to come, then?"

"Rainer thinks he can change my mind and I'm always open to accepting a challenge."

"Well, if he can't change your mind, maybe I can," Gail winked.

"Stop it," Luke warned her. Though he knew the damage had already been done. Very few men were immune to Gail's confident charm. Hayes, with his high-and-mighty attitude and self-professed superior intellect, was bound to be no exception.

Thankfully, their tour guide arrived moments later, sparing Luke and the rest of the crew from having to watch Gail engage in her most misguided romantic endeavor to date.

"Luke Rainer! It's a pleasure to finally meet you. I'm a big fan." The jovial man, dressed in a green and gold plaid kilt and a brown tweed blazer, greeted Luke with a broad grin and a hearty handshake.

"The pleasure is mine, good Sir," Luke replied.

"And is that... Michael Sinclair?" their guide asked. Mikey, never one to make a spectacle of himself, simply waved. "No one told me that you'd be along as well! What an honor. You know, I bought your book for my daughter just a few weeks ago. She's something of a paranormal enthusiast - well, as am I. But she was just beside herself when she found out I'd be spending a few days with the *Cemetery Tours* crew. I can't imagine the look on her face when I tell her that I got to meet you as well!"

"Oh. Well. Thank you," Mikey replied. "I uh... I hope she likes the book."

"Oh, I'm sure she will. I'm sure she will. M'name's Alistair, by the way. Alistair Ervine. And we've a lot to see so without further ado, why don't I start off by telling you about this magnificent palace?" Alistair offered.

"I'm sorry, Alistair, but before you begin, I just want to make sure it's all right with you if we put you on film? I know you spoke with our producers and if I'm not mistaken, you signed the release form, but I just wanted to double check with you," Luke said.

"Thank you, Sir. I appreciate that. Yes, I signed the form and am very much looking forward to being featured on the show. Like I said, I'm a big fan. Not just of *Cemetery Tours*, but anything that can't be explained."

"*Everything* can be explained," Hayes said. "Somehow, someway, there is a rational explanation for everything."

"Hey, you know how you said you didn't want to be on the show? That means ixnay on the audio commentary," Luke told him.

"You're saying I'm not allowed to talk?" Hayes asked.

"That is exactly what I'm saying. Carry on, Alistair."

"Er, right. Thank you, Luke. As I was saying, I'm sure you all know this magnificent palace behind you to be Holyroodhouse Palace. It is Her Majesty's official residence here in Edinburgh and..."

Although Alistair didn't touch too much on the haunted history of the Royal Mile as he guided them along the northbound path that would eventually lead to Edinburgh Castle, Luke always liked to acknowledge the history and acquaint his viewers with wherever they happened to be filming before an investigation. And he knew that his friends would enjoy seeing places like the Parliament building, John Knox's House, and St. Giles' Cathedral.

"Now, from what I understand, you'll be taking an extended tour and investigating Edinburgh Castle tomorrow. Is that correct?" Alistair asked.

"Yes," Luke answered. "And of course, we'd love to have you along. If you're available."

"Wouldn't miss it for the world," Alistair grinned as he checked the time on his pocket watch. "Well, it's a bit early, but what do you say we make our way over to Greyfriars? If you like, we could stop in at the bar. Or better yet, I'll take you across the street to the Elephant House for a coffee or a bite to eat - "

"Or to stage an impromptu *Harry Potter* themed photo shoot outside," Gail grinned.

"Oh, but I didn't bring my wand!" Peter lamented.

"That's okay. You can borrow mine," Gail offered.

"Thanks. You're a pal."

It didn't surprise Luke in the slightest that his friends were completely geeking out over the idea of visiting the Elephant House. It *did* surprise him, however, that Dr. Killjoy Hayes seemed equally excited to experience the magic.

Kate thought so, too.

"Wait a minute. *You're* a *Harry Potter* fan?" she asked as he took his turn posing in front of the sign in the window proudly identifying the Elephant House as the cafe where J.K. Rowling penned her famous series.

"You find that hard to believe?" Hayes smirked.

"Yes," she answered point-blank.

"I'm actually a huge nerd. I love fantasy, science fiction, comic books..."

"And yet you criticize and condemn anyone who believes in ghosts."

"I criticize and condemn anyone who encourages innocent people to put their faith in something that doesn't exist. J.K. Rowling doesn't run around trying to convince her readers that witchcraft is real. She knows and her readers know that her magic exists only in the pages of her books."

"So, you'd rather Michael and Luke not offer people hope?"

"I'd rather them not offer people *false* hope."

"It isn't false."

"I'll be the judge of that," Hayes told her, staring her down and crossing his arms over his chest.

"Well then, judge away," Luke said, "because our next stop is the most haunted cemetery in the world: Greyfriars Kirkyard."

Located in Old Town, Edinburgh, Greyfriars Kirkyard appeared, at first glance, to be a very peaceful place. The day's overcast did nothing to mute the vibrant greens and deep purples of the leaves that fluttered around aged and weathered tombstones. Michael couldn't help but think that the serene setting would be more fit for a fantasy tale rather than a ghost story.

But the further they ventured into the cemetery, and the more Alistair told them of its dark history, the more Michael began to realize that the fairy tale was only a facade. Greyfriars Kirkyard was a scene straight out of a Stephen King novel. Lost memories of plague victims and discarded bodies seeped through the dirt beneath their feet. Stone carvings of angels and demons watched them pass with mournful eyes. Perhaps the most unsettling, however, were the iron bars that rose up out of the ground, forming cage-like structures around several graves.

"To protect the dead from body-snatchers," Alistair explained. "There was a time, back in the 1800s, that corpses were being dug up and sold to medical students at the University of Edinburgh. And I'm not talking about one or two bodies to the odd fellow in your class. It was a regular outbreak. Those iron cages you see are called mortsafes. Families had them erected to protect their loved ones. Keep them in the ground where they belong."

"That... is horrifying," Kate declared, looking pale and more than a little shaken.

"That's the least of your worries here, lass," Alistair told her. "You've yet to hear about *Bluidy* Mackenzie."

"Bloody... Mackenzie?" Michael asked. He wasn't sure if that was a ghost or something worse, but either way, he was certain that he didn't care to meet it.

"Sir George Mackenzie, one of the most active and aggressive spirits ever documented," Luke explained. "The story goes that back in the late 1990s, a homeless man broke into Mackenzie's vault in the middle of the night, seeking shelter and a place to sleep. But when he tried to break into Mackenzie's casket, he fell backward into a sunken chamber, filled with the decayed corpses of plague victims. Horrified, he fled the tomb and was never seen again. But it was too late. By disturbing the resting remains of George Mackenzie, he inadvertently unleashed an entity so dark and so powerful that it's become known around the world as the Mackenzie Poltergeist."

"That's very good, Luke. But I'm afraid that's only half the story," Alistair said. "Sir George Mackenzie was as nasty a piece o' work in life as he's reported to be in death. You see, when King Charles II ascended the throne in the late 1600s, he appointed George Mackenzie to serve as Lord Advocate. As such, he was responsible for prosecuting thousands of Presbyterian Covenanters who refused to swear their loyalty to the King and his church. He had them incarcerated and tortured in what has come to be known as the Covenanters' Prison."

It was only then that Michael realized that they had stopped in front of a padlocked gate. Behind the black iron bars, he saw two trees, guarding a path that stretched back into what Michael first perceived to be a private courtyard. But upon closer inspection, he realized that the walls were made of gravestones and monuments to the dead. A single solemn ghost trudged the perimeter of the prison yard; his face tired, his eyes gazing into nowhere.

Unaware of the Covenanter's presence, Alistair carried on with his story.

"When Mackenzie died in 1691, he was buried in a tomb called the Black Mausoleum..." He directed the group's attention to the cylindrical structure behind him. "A mere stone's throw from the same prison where his victims were tormented, murdered, and laid to rest."

There, standing before the mausoleum, Michael's anxiety skyrocketed. His heart raced. His head spun. His stomach turned. For a few moments, he really thought he was going to have to run to the bushes and puke. He'd never heard of a ghost being able to actually curse someone, but he didn't want to risk it by vomiting on *Bluidy* Mackenzie's front lawn.

But wait.

There was no ghost. Well, except for the poor man pacing the Covenanter's Prison. But he didn't even seem to realize that they were there.

So why was he feeling so drained? It didn't make sense. And yet, he wasn't the only one who'd picked up on something not quite right.

"The energy around here is super dark," Gail observed.

"Aye," Alistair agreed.

"Is it possible that this is, in part, a residual haunting?" J.T. asked.

"A what?" Michael asked.

"Energy left over from significant events," Luke explained. "And I wouldn't be surprised, given this area's history. But as far as George Mackenzie goes, I believe we're dealing with a highly intelligent and highly malevolent spirit. Speaking of, Mikey, any sign of him?"

"No," Michael answered honestly.

"Are you sure? Because I'm with Gail. There is definitely some dark energy here."

"I feel it, too. But there's nothing."

"Imagine that," Hayes remarked.

"Wait a minute, Luke," Kate spoke up. "You said that this entity or spirit is known today as the Mackenzie

Poltergeist. Is it possible that whatever this is isn't fully... you know... human?"

"That is a very real possibility," Luke said.

"This is ridiculous," Hayes laughed and shook his head.

"Hey. Peanut gallery. Zip it."

Michael didn't know how to say it, but he was actually with Hayes on this one. He couldn't deny that ghosts existed. But poltergeists? Inhuman spirits? That was a stretch, even for him.

"Are you sure you don't see anything, Mikey?" Luke asked.

"I'd tell you if I did," Michael answered.

"Well, if he isn't around, you could always summon him," Alistair said.

"How?" Luke asked.

Oh no, Michael thought. *Bad idea. Terrible idea.* Because if there was one thing he'd learned from Luke, it was that if you opened yourself up to the paranormal, if you invited the ghosts in, they would come.

"There was an old rhyme that schoolchildren used to chant at the mausoleum door, taunting Mackenzie, daring him to appear."

"And do you feel comfortable reciting that rhyme? Or would you rather I do it?" Luke asked.

"No, no, it's fine. I've said it at least half a dozen times," Alistair said.

"Has it ever worked?" J.T. asked.

"Can't be sure. I can't see spirits." Alistair grinned at Michael. "I have left, however, with unexplained bruises, scratches. Once, I'd even swear to ya that something followed me out of the graveyard and straight to my house."

"Okay, that is exactly what we don't need," Michael told him.

"Speak for yourself, Mikey. I'm ready to meet this guy. Let him do his worst!" Luke exclaimed. "Alistair, if you would do the honors?"

"It'd be my pleasure."

Michael planted himself firmly in front of Kate and braced himself as Alistair stepped forward and bellowed into the cool Scottish evening:

"Bluidy Mackenzie, come oot if ye dar.
Lift the sneck and draw the bar!"

CHAPTER EIGHT

Nothing.

There was nothing. Just a stirring of leaves and the distant sounds of the busy Edinburgh streets.

Michael heaved a sigh of relief as Kate took his hand.

"Anything?" she whispered.

"No," he replied.

"Are you sure?"

In that moment, Michael felt his blood run cold. He tried to pretend that he hadn't heard the tremble of fear in Kate's voice or noticed the subtle shift of energy in the air. The doors to the Black Mausoleum remained securely shut, but Michael kept his eyes fixed and focused, watching for even the slightest movement.

And then, he saw it. It was barely visible, but it was there: a pale, ghostly face staring out at them through the barred window of one of the mausoleum doors.

Michael tried not to react, but Kate tuned into his sudden apprehension.

"What is it?" she asked, sounding like she wasn't altogether certain that she wanted to know the answer.

"Is he here?" Luke wanted to know. "Do you see him?"

"He's watching us," Michael murmured.

"Awesome!" Luke exclaimed. Then, he glanced back at his team. "You guys ready for this?"

"Oh, yeah," Peter answered.

"Gail? You got the digital recorder?"

"Right here."

"All right. Let's do it." Luke announced, turning back to the mausoleum. "George Mackenzie! We know you're there! Show yourself!"

Michael grimaced. He didn't know a whole lot about this spirit, but he got the dreadful feeling that it did not appreciate being told what to do.

"You know, George, word on the street is you're kind of a dick," Luke continued. "Why don't you come on out here and prove them wrong? Or better yet, prove them right. You want to attack me? Leave scratch marks all over my body? Go ahead."

"Luke, be careful," Kate begged.

But Luke didn't heed her warning.

"Come on, Bloody Mackenzie! What are you hiding from? Are you ashamed? Ashamed of how you treated all those Covenanters? Or do you still think your actions were justified, you evil, cowardly son of a - "

"Urrgh!"

All of a sudden, Gail doubled over, clutching her stomach and clenching her jaw.

"Gail!" J.T. cried out, nearly dropping his camera. "Are you okay?"

"No. My stomach... is killing me," she groaned.

"Seriously, George?" Luke hollered at the mausoleum. "I told you to attack *me*, not my crew! And going after the girl? That is not cool, man."

Michael turned his attention away from Luke and the mausoleum and back to where Gail had crumpled to the ground, pale as a sheet and breathing heavily. She was in no condition to carry on with the investigation, especially with Luke continually taunting and challenging the same spirit that had stricken her.

"Luke, I think that's enough," Michael said.

"Don't worry, Mikey. I know what I'm doing."

"You sure do," Hayes commented.

"And what, pray tell, does *that* mean?" Luke demanded.

"You've really got this whole routine down to an art. And it's a decent act. I'm actually almost impressed. But you know there's nothing behind those doors except dried bones and dusty coffins."

"Oh, ye of little faith," Luke remarked. "Did you hear that, George? This guy doesn't believe that you exist. He thinks this is all just one big hoax. You know, if you want to be remembered for something other than your crimes against the Presbyterians, now's your chance!"

Hayes shook his head.

"I promised you an open mind, Rainer, but I can only suffer this foolishness for so long."

"Well, maybe the spirits can only suffer *you* for so long. Because let me tell you, if I were dead right now, your voice alone would have me hightailing it straight to hell."

"I'm beginning to feel like I'm already there," J.T. muttered.

"You seem like a pretty smart guy," Hayes said to J.T. "I think that's what baffles me the most. Why do you go along with all of this? You could be doing anything with your time and yet you're out here watching Luke Rainer pick fights with his imaginary friends in the middle of a graveyard."

"You know, for a guy who doesn't want anything to do with this investigation, you're awfully chatty..."

It was only then, as Luke and Hayes bickered back and forth, that Michael noticed the figure gliding slowly and steadily across the cemetery grounds. The somber ghost of the middle-aged man walked with purpose, his dark gaze fixed on Luke. Michael felt his stomach drop.

George Mackenzie had emerged from his grave.

"Hey, Luke?" Michael called.

"Not now, Mikey!"

"But - "

"Whoa, whoa. What the hell?" Peter exclaimed, cutting Michael off.

"What's going on?" J.T. asked.

"This camera is completely freaking out. It's freezing... it's glitching and now it's - it's gone. My camera's dead."

"Mine is fine," J.T. said.

"Then keep rolling! Don't stop!" Luke instructed. *Now* he was paying attention. "Mikey, what do you see?"

But before Michael could answer, the world around him began to spin. His eyesight blurred and he broke out into a cold sweat. He knew the sensation all too well. The spirit was draining his energy. Again.

Through the haze, he felt Kate grab his arm, steadying him. He prayed that Mackenzie wasn't affecting her as well.

"He's... behind you..." Michael tried to warn Luke.

It was too late. Unable to move, barely capable of catching his breath, Michael could only watch as Mackenzie raised his hand and, in one swift, fluid motion, struck Luke across the face. Luke didn't flinch. In fact, he didn't seem to feel it at all.

Hayes, on the other hand, was looking just as sickly and shaken as Michael felt. He pressed a hand to his forehead, skewing his glasses, and exhaled slowly through his mouth.

"Looking a little green around the gills there, Hayes. You okay?" Luke asked, still blissfully oblivious to Mackenzie's attack.

"I'm jet-lagged and exhausted," Hayes responded through gritted teeth. He was resisting, and Mackenzie was feeding off of it.

"Are you sure you're not being haunted?"

Hayes never got the chance to answer. He could only whimper, in fear and confusion, as the spirit of George Mackenzie reached out and wrapped both hands around his neck.

"Ow."

"I'm sorry. I know this stings."

"It's not your fault. I just - agh!"

"Are you sure you don't want to go to the hospital?" Kate asked Michael for what she knew seemed like the thousandth time. She'd done her best to nurse the wounds he'd sustained tackling Caleb Hayes to the ground, but she couldn't help worrying that a few of the deeper cuts might require real medical attention.

"I'd really rather not draw any more attention to myself," Michael admitted.

Although Kate didn't necessarily agree with his reasoning, she couldn't say she blamed him, either. After all, *#GreyfriarsSmackdown* had been trending on Twitter for the better part of the evening and already, memes were emerging of Michael knocking Hayes off his feet. For example, someone had labeled Hayes as "ME" and Michael as "MY ANXIETY." It would have been sort of funny, you know, if it were anyone other than the man that she loved.

"Well, if it's any consolation, I thought what you did was very heroic," Kate told him.

While the videos circulating around the internet made it appear that Michael's feud with Hayes had escalated into full-blown violence, the truth was that Michael had thought he was saving Hayes from being choked to death by Bloody Mackenzie. Unfortunately, neither Hayes nor the bewildered teens who happened to witness and film the entire encounter interpreted Michael's actions as any sort of chivalrous.

"I'm just thankful Hayes isn't threatening to sue," Michael muttered.

Kate agreed, though Hayes had made it agonizingly clear that he could and should.

"He should be thanking you," she said, taking a seat next to Michael on their cozy hotel bed. "I still can't believe he's here."

"After getting punched in the face with his university ring... I can," Michael remarked dryly. Kate laughed. Then she ran her fingers through his hair, leaned in, and gently pressed her lips to his. After the kiss ended, Michael took her hand, lacing their fingers together. "Do you think coming here was a mistake?"

"No. Do you?"

"I'm hoping it wasn't," he admitted.

"Look, today was... an off day. But we knew what we were signing on for. Well, most of what we were signing on for, anyway," she acknowledged. "I still think this is going to be an amazing trip."

"Really?"

"It's already the best trip of my life. And that's because I'm here with you." Kate told him. "And because I got my picture taken in front of the Elephant House."

"That's going to end up being the highlight, isn't it?"

"Honestly, I can't imagine anything better than visiting the birthplace of *Harry Potter*," she teased. Michael smiled then; a genuine smile. Then he reached up, cupped her face with a warm hand, and kissed her. His kiss took her breath away. "Okay, maybe one thing." Or two. Or every second spent in his embrace.

Trailing her hands along his shoulders and down his chest, she took his shirt in her grasp and pulled him backward onto the bed. For a moment, neither spoke. They simply shared in the silence and the soft glow of the Edinburgh sunset. Evening light danced across Michael's face, illuminating his handsome features; his sharp jawline, perfect cheekbones, parted lips. Yet even as the sunset kissed every inch of his skin, Kate couldn't help but notice the shadows lingering in his dark eyes.

"What is it?" she whispered.

He hesitated.

"I... I can't get him out of my head."

"Who?"

"Mackenzie. I know that we've been around malevolent spirits before but there's just... something different about this one. It's like... maybe I never fully understood just *how* powerful they can be..."

"He's not here with us now, is he?"

"No. He retreated back to his crypt. And that in itself is unusual. Most of the ghosts I've met don't like to haunt their own graves," Michael commented.

"Yeah, but Mackenzie is buried right next to the Covenanter's Prison, one of the places he felt most powerful in life. And if he's been feeding off of that residual energy, not to mention the fear and excitement of all the tourists who visit the cemetery every day, it's really no wonder he possesses the strength that he does."

While Michael considered what she'd said, Kate nestled herself closer to him and pressed her forehead against his. Finally, he asked, "Do you think it's possible... that there could be more than just ghosts out there?"

"I think anything's possible," Kate answered honestly. "And I think there will always be questions that we can't answer, occurrences that we can't explain. And you know, as mortals, I don't think we're meant to understand everything. Fascination, discovery, mystery... they're all part of the human experience."

"You make it sound so romantic," Michael told her.

"I do," Kate admitted. "I guess I still get swept away by all of it. Don't get me wrong, I was terrified this afternoon. I haven't been that scared in a long time and I'm hoping the rest of our trip is dull in comparison. But it's also been a spectacular adventure and... I wouldn't trade it for anything."

It must have been what Michael needed to hear, because finally, finally he leaned in and kissed her without any inhibition or uncertainty.

In the back of her mind, Kate knew that the hauntings were far from over. Tomorrow would bring about new tales of tragedy and dark discomfort, new attempts to bridge the gap between the world of the living and the world of the dead. Tomorrow could very well take them to hell and then back again.

Even so, Kate decided, tomorrow was going to have to wait.

For the moment, tonight was all that mattered.

CHAPTER NINE

Michael's dreams were plagued with murder. Murder and fear and devastating guilt.

In his nightmare, he and Kate were helping Luke investigate a dark and decrepit hotel where guests had reported being terrorized by demonic activity. While Luke was busy setting up his equipment, Michael led Kate into an empty room and began to kiss her with a sort of raw craving and rabid possessiveness that he never knew he could feel. It was foreign, frightening. But he didn't fight it. He embraced it.

Then Kate broke away from him, claiming she'd heard a pounding in the walls. It wasn't until she pointed it out that Michael noticed it, too.

"Ignore it," he told her. But the noise persisted.

"I'm going to tell Luke," Kate announced. Before Michael could stop her, she disappeared.

As soon as she was gone, dreamlike memories came flooding back to Michael. He had been there before, in that same hotel room. And he'd tortured. And he'd killed. He could see the pale, grimy, dismembered corpses of his victims as clear as day.

No. No, that wasn't me, he tried to convince himself. But to no avail. He was the reason for the hauntings. He'd summoned those demons with the blood he'd spilt. He was to blame. And he sorely regretted it.

Kate couldn't find out. She'd never look at him the same way again. But could he really keep something like this from her? Would he be able to live with himself if he did?

Would he be able to live with himself either way?

"Michael!" Kate's voice cut through the deafening silence.

Past sins momentarily forgotten, he raced out into the hallway just in time to witness Kate and Luke attempting to pry a loose panel away from the wall outside the room.

"I think... I think there's something in here," Luke said.

Finally, the panel broke free, tumbling to the floor in a cloud of dust and ashes. While Kate and Luke both turned away, coughing and sputtering, Michael stepped forward to take a closer look inside the hollow wall. At first, he saw nothing through the cloud of filth. But then, the dust began to clear, settling on the frame of a large wooden box.

A coffin.

It was a coffin.

And I put it there.

As the realization crashed into him, Michael flew into a frenzied panic, stumbling backward and colliding with Kate and Luke.

"Michael, what's wrong?" Kate asked, staring at him with wide, frightened eyes.

"I can't... I don't... I'm sorry."

"It's okay. Just talk to me," she pleaded.

But he couldn't. He couldn't bear it. Confessing what he'd done... that would make it real. And it wasn't real. It couldn't be real.

Please, don't let this be real.

His prayer went unanswered.

Clammy and disoriented with disgust and remorse, Michael watched as Luke climbed into the wall to retrieve the box. It slid out into the hallway with little resistance. It was as though it wanted to be found. And perhaps it did. Or something inside of it did.

Reemerging from the hollow depths of the wall, Luke reached for his discarded pry bar and jammed it underneath the coffin's lid.

"Wait a minute. What are you doing?" Michael asked.

"What do you mean what am I doing? I'm about to crack this baby open!" Luke told him.

"Don't."

"Why not?"

"Just don't!"

"Listen to him, Luke," Kate said.

"You're telling me you're not even the slightest bit curious about - "

KNOCK KNOCK KNOCK!

A sharp rapping from inside the coffin cut him off mid-sentence, startling all three of them.

"What is that?" Kate gasped. "What's in there?"

"Whatever it is," Luke said, "I don't think it's going to be happy to - "

KNOCK KNOCK KNOCK!

"Mikey? Kate?"

... What?

The voice ringing out from inside the coffin was muffled but unmistakably Luke's. But that was impossible. Luke was standing right there. Right beside the coffin. That couldn't be his voice.

"Hellooo? Lovebirds! Rise and shine!"

It was then and only then that Michael finally stirred out of his troubled slumber. Blinking in the hazy morning light, he stretched and shifted to see Kate, fully dressed in jeans and a green blouse, kicking last night's clothes aside as she made her way to the door.

"Hey," she answered, keeping her voice low. "Michael's still asleep."

"Well, tell him to get his skinny ass up. We've got a castle to investigate! And also, I'd like to have a word with him about - Hey, Mikey!" Luke grinned, catching Michael's eye. "So you actually are awake!"

"Sort of," Michael confessed, running a hand through his tousled hair. He didn't want to admit it to either of them,

70

but his head was still spinning from the bizarre dream they'd unknowingly just freed him from.

"Are you feeling okay?" Kate asked.

"Yeah, I'm fine. It's probably the jet lag."

"Or the malevolent spirit that attacked us in the middle of the graveyard. Remember him? Bloody Mackenzie? Speaking of..." Luke let himself inside the room and strode over to the bed. "You didn't happen to catch him scratching my face up or anything, did you?"

In his sleep-induced stupor, Michael hadn't even noticed the three scratch marks glowing an angry red across Luke's face, but sure enough, they were there.

"Um... maybe..." Michael answered.

"Does maybe mean yes?"

"I mean, I saw him take a swipe at you. I didn't realize that he could actually hurt you."

"Seriously? Even after all you've seen and experienced?"

"Remember, Luke, I'm still relatively new to this."

"Fair enough," Luke said. "Well, I am going to leave and let you get ready. No offense, my man, but I'm pretty sure if a ghost walked in right now, he'd be scared of *you*."

"Thanks," Michael deadpanned.

"Don't mention it. Oh, and before I forget, they do serve complimentary breakfast here, so if you want to eat something, go down and grab it. I'm actually headed that way myself. Just please, whatever you do, don't take your time. Alistair is meeting us at Edinburgh Castle in exactly one hour."

"In that case, why don't I go with him and then bring food back to the room?" Kate said to Michael. "That way, I can have breakfast here and waiting for you after you get yourself together."

"Have I mentioned how much I love this woman?" Luke asked. "You're a lucky man, Mikey. Especially considering the state of your hair right now."

"You know, he's right. You have definitely looked better," a new voice declared, joining in on the fun. Michael waited until Kate and Luke were out of the room before he addressed the teenaged ghost in the room.

"Where have you been?" Michael asked Brink.

"Exploring. Playing the tourist. Checking out some of the local haunts. Get it?" Brink's eyes sparkled. He'd clearly been waiting to use that one for a while.

"Hilarious." Michael stretched again and finally lifted himself up and out of bed.

"And hey, listen, I'm sorry I bailed on you. Once Hayes showed up and everyone started yelling at each other..."

"It's all right. I understand," Michael assured him. And he did. Although it was often easy to forget, Brink was still a spirit and spirits thrived on energy. Negative energy would have a negative effect on anyone, but ghosts were particularly susceptible.

"So what did I miss? Did you manage to make a believer out of him? Are you all one big happy ghost-hunting family?"

"Not exactly," Michael answered before telling Brink the whole story.

"You see? That's why I don't hang out in graveyards. Ghosts get reputations and it's douchebags like George McNamara who give all of us a bad name."

"Mackenzie."

"Don't interrupt me. I'm on a soapbox. As a disembodied individual, I think it's time that we had some new representation. Like that one book series that Kate was telling us about. Remember that one? The one where the hot human girl falls in love with the ghost who haunts her bedroom? We need more of that in our society."

"You know, Brink, as much as I empathize, I need to take a shower and get dressed."

72

"Go ahead. I can yell at you through the bathroom door."

"Lucky me."

As much as Michael hoped that Brink was only joking, he wasn't.

"Speaking of romance, are you still planning to pop the question while we're here?" Brink shouted.

"You know, I'm not sure I want to be yelling out the answer to that question when she could be walking through the door literally any second."

"Don't worry, I'm keeping an eye out. So, are you?"

Michael paused to think about it.

"I don't know."

"Why not? Because of Hayes? Don't let *him* stand in your way."

"I'm not letting him stand in my way. I'm trying to decide what would make my future wife happiest."

"If you really wanted that, then you would have gone with one of the rings I suggested. But that's beside the point. You know that Kate is going to say yes to you no matter how, when, or where you propose. So you might as well have the satisfaction of doing it in front of a bitter, single skeptic whose last girlfriend was probably his pillow."

At that, Michael actually threw his head back and laughed. It was the first proper laugh he'd had since they arrived. He had to admit, it felt good. Almost as good as the hot water against his skin as it washed away any remnants of last night's visit to Greyfriars.

"I'll keep that in mind," Michael said.

"As you should. However! You have to swear *on my grave* that you won't propose without me. I *have* to be around. Got it?"

"Got it."

"No, you've got to say it. I would make you spit shake on it but I can't spit. Say it. Oh no, wait! Don't say it! Kate just walked in. And your breakfast looks... interesting... Are those beans? I think those are beans."

Again, Michael found himself snickering to himself. In spite of the events of the last twenty-four hours, from his gruesome dreams to the appearance of the scratches across Luke's face, he found himself feeling oddly optimistic. Maybe they'd already seen the worst of what Scotland's ghosts had to offer.

Maybe today would be everything that yesterday could have been.

Or maybe he was finally going to get that restraining order he'd always figured was inevitable. Granted, he'd been expecting it would be from a haunted neighbor who was tired of waking up to find their books flying off the shelves or a grieving loved one who suspected him of cyberstalking. But a skeptical scholar with aches in his shoulder and bruises around his neck made sense too.

"That's pretty gnarly... Have you looked in the mirror lately?" Luke asked Hayes, eyeing the ugly purple splotches with a grimace.

"Have *you*? What happened to your face?" Hayes wanted to know.

"Got scratched up by a ghost. Same one who tried to strangle you. Pretty cool, huh?"

Hayes shared neither his opinion nor his enthusiasm.

"No one tried to strangle me. If I'm bruised, it's because Michael Sinclair elbowed me in the throat in the throes of his so-called rescue."

"Oh, please. I saw the look on your face! You felt it! You knew something was there!"

"All I know is that you have a troupe of tremendous actors here who will happily sacrifice their own personal integrity for the sake of your fragile ego."

"I'll have you know my ego is anything but fragile," Luke declared.

"I'd drink to that," Gail muttered. "Speaking of, did you know that there's a whisky shop on the Edinburgh Castle grounds?"

"Ooh. Can we go there?" Peter asked.

"Is it haunted?" Luke asked.

"Probably," Gail responded.

"We'll see," Luke said.

"Pft. You never let us have any fun," Gail grumbled.

"What are you talking about? Last night was fun," Luke argued.

"You don't really know what fun is, do you?" Gail asked.

"Yeah, I love everything about what we do, but even I can admit last night was kind of a bummer," Peter agreed. "I haven't felt that drained after an investigation in a long time."

"Well then, I suggest breaking out your sage and cleansing crystals," Luke advised. "Holy water, rosaries, what have you. Then say your prayers and buckle up. Because as far as I'm concerned, we're just getting started."

CHAPTER TEN

Despite its haunted history and Luke's insistence that the grounds were literally crawling with ghosts, Michael had to admit Edinburgh Castle was pretty cool. What he'd seen of it, anyway.

Built atop an ancient volcano called Castle Rock, the fortress itself overlooked the entire city of Edinburgh. And what a spectacular view it was. Michael could see beyond the New Town skyline all the way to the Firth of Forth. Even more breathtaking, however, was the smile on Kate's face as she took in the sights and the city and the life around her.

Worth it, he thought. Her happiness made *everything* worth it.

For half a second, Michael imagined dropping to one knee and asking Kate to marry him right there, right then. With sunlight dancing on the waters of the Firth and pink and white flowers blooming around the castle gardens, it was the perfect setting for a proposal.

Before he could reach into his pocket for the ring, however, Kate threw her arms around his waist, breaking him out of his trance.

"Smile for me!" she instructed, holding her phone up for a selfie. Michael had never cared for the way he looked in pictures, but he did as she said. Then she kissed him on the cheek and snapped a second picture.

Meanwhile, Luke and the crew were filming the Halloween special's introduction while a small swarm of beguiled fans watched with excitement and adoration.

"Prisoners. Witches. A lonely piper. These are just a few of the ghosts that you'll meet in one of the most majestic... and most haunted... countries in the world. Welcome to

Scotland. Here we will - wait a minute. Hey, hold it! Cut!" Luke hollered. "Mikey! Get over here!"

"Why?" Michael asked.

"Call it earning your keep. Now hurry up. We've got a schedule to stick to."

Michael looked down at Kate, hoping she might take pity on him and tell him he didn't have to do anything that Luke said. Instead, she winked and gave him a playful nudge. Realizing he was never going to win as long as Kate and Luke were on the same team, Michael trudged over to where Luke was standing.

"Try to contain your enthusiasm, Mikey," Luke remarked. "Okay, let's roll again!"

While Luke recited his introduction for the camera, Michael's eyes drifted over to where Hayes was attempting to make polite conversation with a few of the fans. Most were brushing him off, preferring to give their favorite ghost hunter their utmost attention. But there were a few who didn't seem to mind.

"... and here with me is my good friend and bestselling author, Michael Sinclair. Are you ready for this, Mikey?"

"Huh...? Oh... yeah. Absolutely."

"Cut," Luke groaned. "Mikey, how many times have you done this?"

"Um... Not a lot."

"That is obvious. Let's do it again."

"Just a reminder, Luke, that we do actually want to see what's inside the castle. You know, like ghosts," Gail commented.

"Fair enough. Moving right along."

"So wait... you're not actually going to use that take, are you?" Michael asked Luke.

"Sure we are. People love a bit of awkwardness. It reminds them that you're a real person. Now, let us venture forth! Alistair, if you would be so kind as to lead the way."

"It would be my pleasure," their friendly tour guide answered. "So, how did all of you fare last night?"

"All things considered, not too bad," Luke replied.

"Speak for yourself," J.T. grumbled. "I wasn't affected physically, but God, I had the most gruesome dreams."

"I did, too," Peter said.

"So did I," Kate added.

Michael felt an odd sense of surprise and relief. So he hadn't been the only one.

"How about you, Hayes? Any weird dreams?" Luke asked.

"You do understand that dreams mean nothing," Hayes said.

"That sounds like a yes."

Hayes didn't dignify that with a response.

Inside, Edinburgh Castle was even grander than its already splendid exterior had led Michael to expect. Growing up, he'd never been one to play pretend. He didn't care for knights in shining armor, the kings they served, or the dragons they slayed. Sure, he'd read a fantasy book or two, but he never daydreamed about what it might be like to live those adventures.

Until now.

Now, standing in the center of the Great Hall, with its chandeliers, scarlet walls, and suits of armor, Michael finally understood.

"Oh, this is amazing," Kate sighed.

"It really is," Michael agreed. "It kind of makes me wonder what all I've been missing."

"What do you mean?" Kate asked.

"I guess I'm just realizing that I don't have any real interests outside of the paranormal. Not that that's really an interest. More like a bizarrely forced lifestyle. Either way, I don't really know who I would be or what I might be doing if the ghosts hadn't been a factor."

"Well, if it brings you any peace of mind, I'm rather fond of who you are," Kate assured him. "But you know, it's never too late to expand your horizons. Look at Val! She just turned thirty, she'd never skated a day in her life, and yet she just joined a roller derby league! And she loves it!"

"So maybe it's not too late for me to learn how to ride a bicycle," Michael grinned.

"I could always teach you," Kate reminded him.

"Maybe I'll take you up on that."

"You should."

"Mikey! Kate! We're moving on! Let's go!" Luke called.

"Sorry!" Kate apologized as they sprinted to catch up with the rest of the crew.

"No worries, Beautiful. Just didn't want to see you get left behind."

"Aw. Why thank you, Luke."

"What can I say? I'm a caring guy. Also, I really need your boyfriend to be keeping a sharp eye out for ghosts. With so many people here, it will probably be difficult to collect a whole lot of solid evidence."

"With so many people here, it'll probably be difficult to even catch a glimpse of a spirit. If they choose to appear at all," Michael said.

"Oh, I'm sure they'll show up," Luke said. "Visitors are constantly reporting cold spots, unexplained footsteps, shadow figures... Some even claim to have felt a burning sensation on their hands and faces."

"Burning?" Kate asked. "That's strange."

"It is," Luke agreed. "Until you find out that hundreds of innocent women were burned as witches here on the grounds of Edinburgh Castle."

"What?" Kate gasped.

"A very dark chapter in our country's long history," Alistair acknowledged. "And one that the spirits won't let us forget. Lady Janet, in particular."

"Who?" Gail asked.

"Poor dear Lady Janet Douglas. Falsely accused of witchcraft by King James V. Her brother was his step-father you see, and the King hated him. Hated the entire Douglas clan. So he ordered Lady Janet and her son be imprisoned and tried as witches."

"That's terrible," Kate frowned.

"What happened to her?" J.T. asked.

"Lady Janet was well-beloved and James knew that very few would convict her. So he had her family and servants tortured until they agreed to testify against her. She was found guilty and burned at the stake... and her young son was forced to watch."

"No wonder she's still here," Gail murmured.

"Tell me, Alistair, would it be asking too much to maybe try to contact her?" Luke asked.

"Not at all. We can settle in and set up in Laich Hall," Alistair answered.

He led them to a new room, open and bright, with an intricately designed ceiling and gilded coats of arms adorning the walls. It was a room fit for royalty, not summoning spirits. But Luke seemed delighted.

"This is the same room where I recorded the voice of the piper boy," he announced.

"Another sad tale," Alistair said.

While Luke and the crew worked hastily to assemble their equipment, Michael and Kate wandered slowly, taking in the details of the room. And, as Luke had requested, keeping an eye out for ghosts. But to Michael's surprise (and utter relief), there were no spirits to be seen.

Then again, he'd thought the same thing last night and look what had happened. But the castle was different. The energy there was different. It was lighter, friendlier. The atmosphere inside the castle made Michael feel alive.

"I don't know if Luke's going to find anything here," Michael confessed quietly to Kate.

"I'm kind of thinking the same thing," she said. "Maybe if we were to come back when it was a little quieter, it'd be a different story."

"Okay, I think we're about finished. Mikey, you ready?" Luke called over.

"What do you want me to do?" Michael asked.

"Help us make contact! Here, you can man the Ovilus," Luke said, holding out what looked to be a small recording device with a digital computer screen.

"What is this?"

"It's sort of like a ghost translator," Peter answered. "It takes spiritual energy and then converts it into phonetic responses. Cool, right?"

"Does it work?" Michael asked.

"You tell us," Gail smirked.

"I would, but there's no one here."

"How convenient," Hayes commented.

"Keep your mouth shut and your mind open," Luke instructed.

"I have an open mind, Rainer. What you want is for me to abandon logic and reason in favor of some paranormal fantasy."

"What do you think we do with all this equipment? Do you think we study electromagnetic fields for fun? This is what we do. We make the illogical logical. We find the reason in everything that reason can't explain."

"You find what you *want* to find. Your eager mind is powerful, Rainer. If it thinks that you're sick, it makes you sick. If it wants to believe in ghosts, it conjures them up out of dust particles and creaking walls."

"God, I can't wait to prove you wrong," Luke muttered. "Pete, are we ready to roll?"

"Ready," Peter affirmed.

"Gail? J.T.?"

"Go for it, Tiger," Gail told him.

"Don't call me that," Luke said. "Okay, everybody quiet. Let's begin." He cleared his throat. Then, speaking gently, he asked, "Lady Janet? Are you here?"

Michael glanced around. They were still alone.

Luke continued.

"Lady Janet, my name is Luke Rainer. I'm sorry about what happened to you. It was wrong and I want you to know that the world knows your story. They know that you were innocent."

After a few more moments of silence, Gail spoke up.

"Considering everything she went through, maybe she'd feel more comfortable communicating with a woman."

"You might have a point," Luke agreed.

Out of the corner of his eye, Michael noticed Hayes rubbing his forehead, undoubtedly out of exasperation. That's when he realized that, for what may have been the first time in his life, he was actually hoping that a ghost would show up.

"Hi, Lady Janet. I'm Gail. I would really love to see you, to talk to you... I know that you see hundreds, maybe even thousands, of people every day. They don't acknowledge you. They don't even seem to know that you're there. But we know. And we want to talk to you. Maybe we can help you. But we need you to give us a sign. Let us know that you can hear us."

"Mikey, anything?" Luke asked.

"No," Michael replied. "She's not here."

"Well, it is a big castle," Alistair reminded them. "There is always the chance that you'll find her elsewhere."

But they didn't. Nor did they encounter any of the other ghosts that reportedly walked the grounds of Edinburgh Castle. Not in the Crown Room. Not in St. Margaret's Chapel. Not even in the dungeons that once held American prisoners of war.

It may have been the hustle and bustle of countless tourists, or perhaps, like Brink, the spirits had been repelled by the negative, chaotic energy that Caleb Hayes seemed to thrive on. Either way, as they bid the historic fortress farewell, Michael couldn't help but feel that he'd somehow let everybody down. Kate. Luke. The crew. The spirits.

And, much to his surprise, himself.

CHAPTER ELEVEN

"Okay, so Edinburgh Castle was a royal bust. But fret not, dear viewers. For tonight, we visit the South Bridge Vaults," Luke declared, live-streaming once again for his devoted fans. "Alistair, what can you tell me about these historic vaults?"

"That's a very good question, Luke," Alistair smiled, totally hamming it up for the camera. "Known as the Underground City, the vaults were constructed in the late 1700s and for a while, operated as marketplaces, workshops, even living spaces. But after three decades of poor ventilation and overcrowding, the merchants moved out and the dregs moved in. The vaults became a hotspot for illicit activity; prostitution, theft, even murder."

Kate shuddered, imagining dark streets of death and despair. Although she was eager to explore the nefarious Underground City, a part of her couldn't help but wonder why. It made no sense that she, or anyone really, would be drawn to a place with such violent memories.

Yet, there they stood, outside what appeared to be a simple city archway, preparing to make their descent into Edinburgh's infamous caverns.

Heart racing, she clasped Michael's hand and glanced up at him. He was so lost in his own thoughts that barely responded to her touch.

"Are you okay?" Kate asked him. "What are you thinking about?"

His gaze lingered on the threshold in front of them for a few moments longer before he finally answered.

"How easy it would be to just... run away. To spend the evening dancing with you in one of the local pubs or wandering the aisles of an antique bookshop. We don't have to be here. We could be anywhere..."

"But you want to stay," Kate concluded, detecting the catch in his voice.

"I shouldn't. I should be dragging you away from a place like this. Not escorting you in."

"Well, if it makes you feel better, I want to stay, too. This is the reason we're here, after all."

"One of the reasons." Michael must have been thinking out loud because he blushed and cleared his throat as soon as he realized he'd spoken.

"Okay, team. Let's do this," Luke announced in a tone much quieter and more reserved than his typical speaking voice. Then, he turned and followed Alistair down into the depths of the city.

Inside the tunnels, the refreshing and reassuring light of day gave way to a world of perpetual night. Every step they took echoed in the dreary darkness as old-fashioned lamps and open candles cast dancing shadows across the cavern walls.

"So Alistair, who can we expect to meet down here?" Gail asked.

"There are reports of ghostly cobblers, aristocrats, a shaggy dog, a watcher... But the most infamous spirit is that of a gentleman known as Mr. Boots."

"Mr. *Boots*?" Hayes snickered. "Sounds like something my grandmother would name her cat."

"Don't let the name fool you. This entity is powerful and very aggressive. It's said that he hates intruders and he expresses that hatred by lashing out, shoving visitors, even throwing rocks at them."

"I'm sorry, all that and they still couldn't come up with anything better than *Mr. Boots*?" Hayes asked.

"From what I've heard, he's called that because heavy footsteps are often heard when he manifests," Luke explained.

"Footsteps in an underground echo chamber. Imagine that."

"Heavy, *unexplained* footsteps."

Hayes simply shook his head.

It wasn't until an empty silence began to settle in that Kate realized just how chilled the air had become... and how very not alone she suddenly felt.

Of course you're not alone, she tried to reason with herself. *You're with Michael. You're with the whole group.*

Still, she couldn't shake the feeling that someone unseen had joined their entourage. It wasn't a threatening presence, but one that certainly strived to make itself known. And it was close. So close that it was raising the hairs on the back of her neck and electrifying her fingertips with icy tingles.

"Michael," she whispered.

"Hmm - oh..." The look on his face confirmed what she already knew. That look, however, wasn't one of horror. Mild surprise, perhaps. But nothing dreadful. "Hello."

"Who is it?" Kate asked.

"Kate? Mikey?" Luke interrupted. "Something going on back there?"

"We've just... We've made a new friend," Michael answered.

"Would that be a ghost friend or more like a sewer rat friend?"

"He's a little boy," Michael told him. Then he knelt down and asked, "What's your name?"

"Hold it!" Luke announced, shoving his way past Hayes and his crew, back to Kate and Michael. "Here," he said, handing the Ovilus to Kate. "Watch this for me."

"Okay," Kate said.

"Jack. It's nice to meet you, Jack. My name is Michael." Michael introduced himself and then paused to listen. "This is

Kate." He glanced back up at her. "He likes you. He says you feel warm."

"He can feel me?" she smiled.

"He's holding your hand," Michael told her.

Kate looked down at her frozen fingers. She couldn't see the child, but she knew, beyond the shadow of a doubt, that he was there.

"It's nice to meet you, Jack," Kate smiled.

"**Friend**." The device in Kate's hand spoke in an automated voice.

"He wants to know if you would be his friend," Michael translated.

"Of course," Kate replied.

"So this is the new tactic?" Hayes asked. Everyone ignored him.

"J.T., Pete, get the cameras over here. Gail, take as many still photos as you possibly can," Luke commanded quietly. Then, he knelt down beside Michael. "Hey, Jack. Have you ever been on TV before?"

"Luke, he uh... he doesn't know what TV is," Michael told him.

"Oh, right. Okay. That makes sense," Luke said. "Jack, can you tell me how old you are?"

"**Years**," the Ovilus answered.

"He's seven years old," Michael said.

"Seven. That's a good age," Luke grinned.

"Oh. Um. I don't know. I'm sorry," Michael apologized. Then he explained, "Jack was wondering if we knew where his mother is."

"Oh, sweetheart..." Kate felt her heart breaking for the little boy. Was that why he'd latched onto her? He was hoping she could take him to his mother?

"**Frightened**."

"Can I see that?" Hayes asked, indicating the Ovilus.

"I'd rather you didn't," Luke said. "Oh, and friendly reminder, every time you speak equals like, three more hours of editing for us."

"Forgive me."

"And there you go again," Luke muttered.

"No, no, Jack. It's not you, I promise," Michael said.

"What's wrong?" Kate asked.

"He's overwhelmed. He's not used to having so many people talking around him."

"It's okay, Jack," Kate assured him.

"Luke. Look at this," Gail spoke up.

"Did you get something?"

"A white mist. Right there next to Kate." She held up her small point-and-shoot camera for Luke to see.

"Holy shit, that's amazing, Gail!" Luke exclaimed, zooming in on the photograph.

"Language," Kate scolded.

"What?" Luke asked. "Oh, right. Sorry, Jack. Hey, want to see what you look like on camera?"

"For God's sake, there is *nothing there!*" Hayes burst out.

"Oh yeah? Then explain this!" Luke declared, shoving the camera in Hayes' face. "See that? That mist figure right there? That's Jack."

"That is a lens flare," Hayes argued.

"Okay. Then explain the Ovilus. Explain to me how that device hasn't said a word all day until Jack showed up."

"You've either programmed it - "

"Can't."

" - or Miss Avery is over there typing in the words - "

"Again, can't."

"Nevertheless, that box proves nothing."

"That box proves everything! Michael heard him speak with his own ears. And his words matched the ones produced by the Ovilus!"

"You don't get it, do you? For that argument to be even sort of valid, I would first have to believe that Sinclair is capable of communicating with the dead. And, as you may recall, I don't."

"Okay, you know what? You can believe what you want. I don't care. But please, I'm asking you just this once to play along," Michael pleaded.

"Why? Give me a reason."

"Because Jack is confused and alone and he doesn't understand what's happened to him."

"Really? You'd think after a century or two, he'd at least figure out that he doesn't have a pulse."

"He's just a kid!"

"He. Does not. *Exist.*"

That's when Kate felt it: a fresh surge of fear and agonizing sadness that shook her to her very core. And then... there was nothing. Just the flickering of candlelight and a heavy stillness in the air.

Jack was gone.

As soon as she realized it, Kate felt herself choking back tears. He had come to her. He had felt safe with her. And she'd let him down. She couldn't protect him.

"Wait, what just happened?" J.T. asked.

"The energy shifted. We didn't lose him, did we?" Luke asked.

"Yeah, he's gone," Michael confirmed, rising slowly to his feet.

Luke whirled around to glare at Hayes.

"Are you happy now?" he demanded. "That was probably the first human interaction that kid has had in God knows how long and you scared the hell out of him!"

"I can't believe you still think you're going to make me feel bad. It is literally baffling to me," Hayes remarked, crossing his arms across his chest.

"You listen to me, you arrogant toerag," Luke growled. "When I invited you, we agreed that this would be a *positive* experience and I don't think you need me to tell you that so far, it has been anything but. You are now officially interfering with our investigation, and to top it all off, you're being a huge dick about it."

"I'm not trying to be disrespectful. I'm trying to push you, to *challenge* you. You seem to have it in your head that you can snap a few distorted photographs and have Sinclair parrot some mindless machine and abracadabra, I'll be convinced. But it isn't that simple and it sure as hell isn't that easy. I need undeniable, concrete proof. Not evidence. *Proof*."

No sooner had he spoken the words than the atmosphere inside the vaults shifted again. This time, however, it wasn't a mild chill in the air or the curious energy of a young, innocent boy. No, whatever was approaching was older, intelligent. And it was aggressive.

Very aggressive.

Trembling, Kate reached for Michael's arm. He stepped forward to shield her almost immediately, but his gaze remained fixed and set on something behind Luke and his crew.

"Well, maybe this will be proof enough for you," Michael muttered darkly, drawing in a shaky breath.

Kate's mind flew into a frenzy and her heart thudded with dread. She wanted to turn and flee, but she knew in the back of her mind that whoever or whatever this entity was, it couldn't be outrun. They had wandered willingly into its domain. It was everywhere.

And then, she heard it.

It was quiet, but it was there.

The unmistakable sound of boots, drawing ever closer, echoing on cold cobblestone.

CHAPTER TWELVE

For a split second, Michael truly believed that the menacing figure looming over Luke was part of the tour; an actor paid to dress up in eighteenth-century boots and waistcoat and scare the daylights out of unsuspecting tourists. He may have even believed it for a few blessed moments longer... had it not been for the eyes.

Those ghastly, unseeing, milky-white eyes.

And while the sight of those eyes in that old, craggy face cut through Michael like a broken knife, he found unexpected solace in the realization that the spirit couldn't see him.

"I know you are here," the dead man spoke in a deep, raspy voice. "GET OUT."

"**Out**," the Ovilus repeated.

"What's happening, Mikey?" Luke asked.

Michael was too distracted to answer. Mr. Boots was on the move and Michael wasn't about to tear his eyes away from him for even a second.

"I can hear you," the spirit growled. "I want you OUT!"

"**Out**," the Ovilus spoke again.

"It's him," Alistair announced. "He's here."

"Who? Mr. *Boots*?" Hayes sniggered.

At the sound of his alias, the ghost gave a ferocious, feral snarl. Michael flinched and took an involuntary step back. At the same time, a small rock flew through the air and ricocheted off of the wall, striking Hayes in the leg.

"Ow. Hey, watch it, Sinclair," he snapped.

"It wasn't him," J.T. said.

"How do you know?"

"Because I just caught that pebble on my night-vision camera, and it flew in from clear across the opposite side of the vault."

"It did? Let me see that!" Luke exclaimed. He hovered over his friend's shoulder as the latter replayed his recording. "Oh man, look at that! There it is! Mikey, are you seeing any of this?"

Unwilling to alert the spirit to his whereabouts, Michael simply nodded.

Luke was not impressed.

"That's it? That's all you've got? A nod?"

Michael cast him a wary glance and prayed that Luke would get the message and shut the hell up.

But of course, that didn't happen.

"Okay, what I'm getting from this is that there *is* a ghost down here and it's either sworn you to some bizarre oath of silence or it's so terrifying that it has literally struck you dumb. Which is it?"

Michael held up one finger.

The first.

Luke stared at him.

"You've got to be kidding me."

Hayes, on the other hand, seemed wildly amused.

"Running out of tricks, are we, Sinclair?" he smirked.

"Michael, what's going on?" Kate asked.

Oh, how to explain? After a year of professing that it wasn't the ghosts that scared him, how was he supposed to tell his friends that the specters of Scotland were leading him to question everything he thought he knew about the human spirit and what happened after death? These spirits didn't seem human at all. They were dark, hostile, and inordinately powerful.

"You know what, Mikey? If you want to play charades, you go right ahead. I'm going to try to make contact," Luke said, reaching into his backpack for his digital recorder. "Mr. Boots, is that you?"

The spirit swore at Luke and another rock hurtled across the cavern.

"Something tells me this guy is not happy," Peter remarked.

"This is what he does," Alistair explained. "We're in his territory. And he doesn't like visitors."

"So you toss a few rocks at us?" Luke asked. "That's really all you've got, Mr. Boots? Come on. You can do better than that. Prove to me that you're here!"

With another aggravated groan, the spirit lunged forward, towards Luke's voice, and shoved. Luke, unaware of the spirit's force, stumbled to the side but managed to catch himself before he fell.

"Whoa. Was that you?" Luke asked. "Did you just shove me?"

"I said get *out!*" Mr. Boots shouted.

"**Out**," the Ovilus echoed for the third time.

"I think your rigged computer box is broken," Hayes remarked.

Luke ignored him.

"Mr. Boots, listen to me. I know you've been down here in the dark for a long time. I know you've probably wondered why you're still here after everyone you've known and loved has moved on. We'd like to help you figure that out, or at least get to know you a little better. We just want to talk to you. What do you say?"

Mr. Boots swore again. This time, the Ovilus repeated it.

The entire crew stared at the device.

"Um... have you ever heard it use that word before?" Kate asked.

"No, that's definitely a first," J.T. answered.

"Still thinking it's rigged, Hayes?" Luke asked.

"Yes."

"Are you serious? Even after *that*?"

"All that proves is that you're not above using crude language to try and shock me," Hayes retorted.

"That word still shocks you? I thought you were old enough to have a doctorate."

By now, Hayes was gritting his teeth, and the already agitated spirit was feeding on that frustrated energy. And as he grew stronger, the ground began to tremble beneath their feet.

"Do you feel that?" Gail asked.

"What's happening?" Kate gasped.

"Oh, my God. We're gonna be buried alive," Peter groaned.

And with that admittedly terrifying thought, Michael finally found his voice.

"We need to leave."

"Ah! He speaks!" Luke exclaimed. "Nice of you to join the conversation, Mikey."

"Luke, I'm serious. Let's go."

"With the amount of activity we're getting down here? Are you insane?"

"These aren't normal circumstances."

"Of course not. They're *paranormal* circumstances."

"No." Michael pressed a hand to his forehead. He could feel a migraine coming on. Whether it was due to stress or the work of the spirit, however, he couldn't say. "Listen to me. I don't think we're safe here."

"Mikey, if you were making a damn bit of sense, then I might consider listening to you. But you've barely been able to string two words together since this guy showed up and now you're expecting us to just drop everything and leave what may very well be one of the most intense and important investigations of our career?"

"I promise I will explain everything once we're out of here - " Michael began, but Luke cut him off.

"No. I want to hear it now."

"Yeah, Sinclair. Let's hear it," Hayes smirked. "You couldn't seem to shut up about that imaginary kid. What makes this figment so different?"

"I told you. I'd rather not say down here," Michael said.

"Why? Because you can't think of a reason?"

"No."

"Because you're a fraud?"

"No!"

"Because you're finally realizing that you can't win this one? That no matter what you say or do, you will never be anything more than a lying, manipulative - "

"He's blind!" Michael shouted.

And that's when all hell broke loose.

Luke had always considered himself a man of few regrets. He figured that regrets only served as anchors to tie you back and hold you down. Over the years, he'd made some admittedly questionable decisions, but never once had he regretted making them.

That being said, in the moment that the crew's incredibly expensive video camera, filled with exceptionally valuable footage, flew out of Peter's hands and exploded against the cavern wall, Luke found himself regretting everything. He regretted provoking the spirit. He regretted questioning Mikey's request.

And he sorely regretted ever inviting Caleb Hayes to join them in Scotland.

"Shit!" he cried out, dropping to his knees, desperately trying to reassemble the shattered remains of their camera. "Shit, shit, shit!"

"Oh, my God. Oh, my God," Gail panted over and over again, pressing a trembling hand over her heart.

"How did that - I mean... Did you see how that...?" Peter stammered. "I swear to God, I have no idea how that happened. I had it in my grip, you know? It was there. And then... I've never felt anything like it. It was just *snatched*."

"It wasn't your fault," J.T. assured him.

"Luke, man, I'm so sorry," Peter apologized.

"Don't worry about it," Luke muttered. But his words were empty, his sentiment hollow. His heart thudded and his ears rang, not because of any sort of paranormal attack, but because he knew in the back of his mind that they'd just lost half of their evidence.

For the first time since their descent down into the Edinburgh Vaults, the atmosphere inside the Underground City was deathly still and silent. No one spoke. Even Hayes had sobered up.

Taking several deep breaths, Luke finally stood.

"So... is he gone?" he asked.

"Yeah," Mikey breathed.

"And that's why you were acting so weird? Because he couldn't see?"

Mikey simply nodded.

"That makes no sense," Gail remarked.

"If you had seen him, trust me, it would," Mikey responded. "I'm sorry, Luke."

If Luke had been in even a slightly better mood, he would have taken the opportunity to make a huge deal out of what he was fairly certain was the first time Mikey had ever apologized to him in the history of their friendship. As it so happened, however, he was too busy wracking his brain, trying to figure out how they were supposed to film a two-hour episode with only one working video camera.

"It's fine," Luke answered automatically. "We uh... We should probably get out of here. Sorry, Alistair. I hate to cut the tour short but..."

"No, no, I understand," Alistair assured him. "Mr. Boots, he... he takes a toll."

"That he does," Luke agreed.

Hayes, meanwhile, shook his head and sighed.

"I just don't understand it," the soon-to-be former skeptic muttered.

"You mean seeing a camera sail halfway across a haunted cavern? Yeah, it will probably take some time for you to really process something like that," Luke commented.

"No," Hayes said. "What I don't understand is why a member of your crew would willingly sacrifice expensive equipment just to pull off some ill-conceived stunt."

"Wait, you think I did that on purpose?" Peter demanded.

"Caleb, you're cute, but you *really* need to get a clue if you think that's how we operate," Gail snapped. "Come on, let's get out of here."

And with that, Gail, Peter, and J.T. turned away, following Alistair back up to the streets of Edinburgh and leaving Luke alone with Mikey and Kate.

And Hayes.

"Look, if it really was an accident, then I'm sorry about your camera," Hayes said.

"Gee, thanks. I feel so much better now," Luke spat.

"Believe it or not, Rainer, I'm not the jackass that you think I am."

"Really? What kind of jackass are you, then?"

"I'm choosing to ignore that because you've had a rough night."

"Oh, please don't take the high road," Luke begged.

"I can't help it. I'm the bigger person," Hayes retaliated. Then, his expression softened. "I'll go if you want me to."

"Go?" Kate asked.

"Leave. Go back home to Oregon. I think that having me here is - "

"No," Luke interrupted. "Believe me, letting you leave now would be the easiest thing in the world. A huge part of me wishes you *would* leave. But if you go, it means that you win."

"This isn't a competition, Rainer."

"Let me rephrase it then. If I let you leave now, it means that I've given it all I've got. It means I no longer care enough to try to change your mind. It means that I surrender. And I don't. Not by a long shot. And neither does Mikey. Right, Mikey?" Luke asked, glancing at his friend.

"Um..." Mikey hesitated.

Of course. Perfect. The reluctant medium was tongue-tied. Again.

"He agrees with me," Luke translated.

"I don't know, Luke. Maybe it *would* be better," Mikey said.

"No. No, no, no. You do *not* believe that," Luke told him.

"Hey, if it makes the two of you feel any better, you have successfully creeped me out on more than one occasion. I will admit to that," Hayes said.

"Okay, so what I'm hearing is that you're halfway to investing in a Ouija board. And *that's* why I can't let you leave yet," Luke said. "Besides, I've become fairly adept at reading people over the years, and there's one thing that you're not admitting to anyone. Not even yourself."

"And what is that?" Hayes asked.

Luke smirked. Finally, he had the upper hand.

"You don't want to leave."

CHAPTER THIRTEEN

The world around them brightened considerably the next morning. Kate and Michael, along with the rest of the crew, had spent one last night in Edinburgh before packing their bags and making preparations to head for the Highlands. Although Kate wished that they could have seen more of the city, she was all too eager to leave the ghosts of Edinburgh behind.

"All right, now that we're all settled, here is our itinerary for the day," Luke announced once they had all loaded onto their tour bus. "It will take us approximately three hours to reach Inverness. Once we're there, we'll stop for lunch, enjoy a few hours in town - for the record, I will be hopping around the local electronic stores, shopping for a new camera - and then we'll be having a good, old-fashioned campout right on the shores of Loch Ness."

"Please tell me we get to stay in one of those fancy pod things," Gail remarked.

"How do you expect to catch a glimpse of Nessie from a pod?" Luke asked.

"Oh, dear Lord," Gail groaned.

"So... what *will* we be staying in?" Michael asked.

"Tents!" Luke exclaimed. "We have two sturdy, five-person tents. Perfect for a ragtag group of paranormal enthusiasts in search of the unknown."

"Or perfect for catching pneumonia because it's freezing out here at night," Gail argued.

"Yeah, I don't believe I signed up for a slumber party," Hayes remarked.

"Wow, what a bunch of spoilsports. Where's your sense of adventure?" Luke asked.

"I like tents," Peter grinned.

"I do too," Kate added. Even though she'd technically never actually slept in a tent that wasn't made of blankets and coffee tables, she'd always wanted to have that experience.

"I can sleep anywhere," J.T. said.

"And Mikey will want to stay close to Kate. There you go. The ayes have it!" Luke declared.

Gail huffed but made no further argument.

While most of her companions, Michael included, closed their eyes and dozed through their journey into Inverness, Kate stayed awake the entire time, watching the Scottish countryside pass by her window. There was so much to see, so much beauty to take in, and she didn't want to miss a moment.

As Luke had indicated, they arrived in Inverness shortly before one o'clock. Their first stop was a local pub, The River Tavern. Looking around, Kate imagined it was the sort of place that would be packed to the rafters in the evening. In the early hours of the afternoon, however, the tavern was almost empty.

After indulging in a sumptuous Scottish salmon and a serving of sticky toffee pudding for dessert, Kate and Michael slipped away from the rest of the group to spend at least a few hours together before the campout.

Originally, Kate had intended to simply play the tourist and enjoy the atmosphere of Inverness with the man she loved, but it wasn't long before she found herself gravitating toward the shops.

"I just want to look around," she assured Michael.

"Looking around" the cutest stores in Inverness, however, turned out to be even more hazardous than venturing down into the Edinburgh Vaults. With all the scarves and coffee mugs and t-shirts and magnets, Kate knew she wouldn't make it out alive... without spending at least seventy pounds.

"Okay, I need to get this Stewart crest magnet for my mom. Her grandmother's maiden name was Stewart. For my dad? Oh, definitely this baseball cap with the Scottish flag. Gavin? Eh. He doesn't need anything. Although, he might get a kick out of these Loch Ness shot glasses and - oh! Oh, my God, this mug! Look at this mug! It has Nessie on it!" Kate exclaimed, holding up the mug for Michael to see even though she knew full well that he had a clear view of it from where he stood. "Oh, my God. I have to get this mug."

"Who's the mug for?" Michael asked.

"Me."

"Ah."

"And what about you? What are you going to get?" Kate asked.

"I really don't need anything," Michael told her.

"Not true. You journeyed all this way. You have to at least get *something*. What about a scarf? You would look *so* cute in a tartan scarf. Sinclair is Scottish, isn't it? I bet they have your family tartan!"

And sure enough, they did. It was one of the prettier ones too, one that made Michael look like he should be sitting by a cozy fireplace, sipping tea, and reading an old, well-loved book.

"I am absolutely buying that for you," she announced.

"You don't have to. I'll buy it," he told her. "And actually, I think I'll get two. One for me, one for my mom."

"Aw, that's so sweet. She'll love it." Kate smiled and kissed him on the cheek. Then on the lips. By then, Michael was grinning, too.

"Don't tell Luke, but this is so much better than ghost-hunting."

"Your secret's safe with me," Kate promised. "But you know, I think tonight really will be a lot of fun."

"As long as I get to stay with you."

"You mean you don't want to share a tent with Luke and Hayes?" Kate teased.

"I'd rather share a tent with an actual lake monster."

"Which we may very well discover tonight."

"God, can you imagine what discovering the Loch Ness Monster would do to Luke's ego?" Michael groaned. Kate couldn't help it. She threw her head back and laughed. Then, Michael looked to his left and said, "I don't know. Have you ever tried it?" Kate raised a curious eyebrow. "Brink wants to know if he can swim," he explained.

"That's an interesting question. Any particular reason, Brink?"

"He says that if anyone is going to discover Nessie, it's going to be him because he can't drown. But he doesn't know if he'll actually be able to swim or if he'll just float along on top of the waves."

Kate laughed, imagining Brink bobbing around Loch Ness like a buoy. Michael chuckled, too. Encouraged by his smile, she wrapped her arms around his waist and gazed up at him.

"It's so good to see you happy," she said. "I know the last two days were rough, but I hope that you're still glad we came."

"I am..."

"But...?"

"It's strange," he confessed. "I've spent most of my life trying to convince everyone that I'm completely normal. You know, that I *can't* see dead people. Now I'm in this bizarre situation where I'm actively trying to prove that I can... and it's not working."

"It will," Kate promised. "It's hard to make someone believe in something that they don't understand. It's particularly hard when that someone comes with a doctorate and an IQ that's probably higher than yours and mine put together."

That got another chuckle out of him.

"The weirdest part is that this time last year, I would have been thanking Hayes on bended knee for trying to discredit me."

"I know. And that's why, no matter what happens, I couldn't be prouder of you."

Then, with one last quick kiss, she took his hand and led him across the aisle to the display stocked with souvenir t-shirts.

Five shops and seven purchases later, Michael and Kate met back up with Luke and the crew inside The River Tavern.

"And just where have you two lovebirds been?" Luke asked.

"Shopping. We bought you a hat," Kate announced, dropping the dark navy ball cap onto Luke's head. Adorning the cap were the words *I Believe* and a small, embroidered Nessie.

"Aw, this is perfect! Thanks, guys!" Luke grinned, inspecting his present.

"It was Kate's idea," Michael said.

"As most good ideas are," Luke acknowledged. Then, he rose up off of his bar stool and clapped his hands together. "All right, now that we're all present and accounted for, let's go and find us a monster!"

Try as he might to muster up the appropriate level of enthusiasm, Michael must have failed, because while Kate the rest of the crew scampered to the bus, Hayes fell into step beside him, looking equally indifferent.

"Not crazy about camping, Sinclair?" he asked.

"Not exactly."

And in an odd and totally unexpected moment of camaraderie, Hayes nodded.

"That makes two of us."

The drive to Loch Ness was short, only about thirty minutes. Nowhere near long enough to sell Michael on the whole camping thing. He had to admit, however, there was something very enchanting about Scotland's most famous Loch. Crystal blue waters, guarded by emerald green mountains, kissed the clouds on the horizon while scattered sunlight shimmered on the surface of the waves.

Maybe tonight wouldn't be so bad after all.

"Okay!" Luke exclaimed. "Next item of business. Who knows how to pitch a tent?"

"I do not!" Peter declared.

"That is *not* helpful!" Luke mimicked his friend's eager tone.

"I don't, but I'm willing to learn," Kate offered.

"That's a little better, but still not what I'm looking for," Luke said.

"I know," J.T. finally admitted.

"Ding, ding! We have a winner!" Luke pointed at J.T. "Okay, you and I will set up tents. Kate, if you'd like to lend a helping hand, that would be awesome. Peter, Gail, I definitely need the two of you recording this experience. Mikey, as always, be on the lookout for anything unusual. And Hayes? I don't care what the hell you do. Go collect firewood or something."

"No," Hayes deadpanned.

"Are you sure you don't want me helping with the tents?" Michael asked.

"Assistance is always appreciated, but I'd much rather have you on Nessie patrol," Luke replied.

"You do know that I can't just will mythical beings into existence, right?"

"Not with that attitude, you can't."

Okay, so it *was* going to be a long night.

The pitching of tents actually went smoother than Michael expected. Agreeing on sleeping arrangements, however, was a whole other matter entirely.

"I think we should have a guys' tent and a girls' tent," Gail announced.

"No way is that fair. There are only two of you!" Peter argued.

"Exactly, and we don't want to share a tent with a bunch of smelly guys."

"Excuse you, we smell delightful."

"I'd actually like to be with Michael, if that's all right," Kate said.

"Of course it is. He's your person," Luke said. "However, that does not mean that you get a whole tent all to yourselves. It's not like you're on your honeymoon." Michael hoped that Kate didn't read too much into the cheeky grin on Luke's face. "Since you two are here as my guests, I'll stay with you. J.T. and Pete, you get the skeptic. Gail, you can sleep wherever you want."

"Great. I'm renting a pod."

"No, you're not."

"Fine," Gail sighed. "I guess I'll stay with the guys. I can cuddle up with the skeptic."

"That is the wrong answer. You're staying with us," Luke said.

"But you said I could choose!"

"Yes, and now I am revoking those privileges. You're with us. Deal with it."

"Tell her if she wants, she can cuddle up with me," Brink announced, appearing out of nowhere.

"Not a chance," Michael responded automatically.

"Sorry, Mikey, what was that?" Luke asked.

"Oh. Uh... nothing," Michael answered.

"Is there a ghost here? Is it Brink?" Gail asked.

"Aw, she remembers my name," Brink grinned.

"Brink?" Hayes asked.

"Michael's best friend," Kate explained.

"Let me guess. This friend is a ghost," Hayes drawled.

"What gave me away? Is it the fact that he can't see me?" Brink remarked.

Michael snickered.

"Hey, Brink, why don't you stick around tonight?" Luke asked. "We could conduct a few lakeside experiments. See if we can prove to old Hayes here that you exist."

"Oh, hell yeah!" Brink answered.

"He says yes," Michael translated.

"Excellent! In that case, I'd better make sure all equipment is ready, all batteries are charged. J.T., I know you've done this before, so why don't you get a fire going? The rest of you can start unloading the food. I have about fifteen grocery bags and three coolers full of potatoes, vegetables, chicken, beef... You name it, I probably bought it. And then, get ready. I have a feeling this will go down as one of the greatest nights in paranormal history."

CHAPTER FOURTEEN

Luke hadn't been joking when he claimed that he'd filled fifteen grocery bags with food for the campout. Not only had he purchased anything and everything that they could possibly want for dinner, he'd also grabbed oatmeal, apples, strawberries, and four kinds of coffee for them to prepare in the morning.

"Dude, I thought we were only going to be out here one night. This could last us a week!" Peter commented, eyeing Luke's seemingly endless supply of food.

"Hey, there are seven of us. I wanted to make sure we had enough."

"I get that, but you really didn't have to buy two different kinds of ketchup."

"One is low-sodium."

"Who's watching their sodium?"

"You never know."

While Peter and Luke bantered back and forth over condiments, Michael wandered over to where Kate and Gail stood on the shore, gazing out at the Loch.

"So, you really don't think she's out there?" Kate was asking.

"No. Do you?"

"I like to believe she could be."

"Luke doesn't actually think we're going to see her tonight. He just has it in his head that viewers will enjoy watching us try to rough it in the Scottish wilderness."

"You don't?"

"I think it feels... I don't know, sort of scripted. When we communicate with spirits, it's always so real, so raw. But this? This is just gimmicky."

Kate shrugged.

"Maybe. But you know, as a viewer, I love watching behind-the-scenes videos and seeing my favorite celebrities just hanging out, having fun. I think people will actually really enjoy this segment."

"You're a very positive person, aren't you?"

"I try to be. But I definitely have my moments. Believe me."

"Is that true, Michael?" Gail asked, glancing over at him. "Does she have her moments?"

"Not very often," Michael answered. "And when she does, she usually has a pretty good reason."

"What about the time Gavin dragged the two of you to his girlfriend's production of *Les Mis*? She bitched about that for a solid week," Brink reminded him.

"Do you blame her? That play was *terrible*," Michael said.

"Is he talking about *Les Mis*?" Kate demanded.

Brink threw his head back and laughed.

"It makes her so angry! It's so *funny*," he howled.

Meanwhile, Kate said, "Please ask Brink why he's trying to ruin my magical evening by resurrecting such awful memories."

Now Michael was snickering, too. He didn't want to upset her, but he had to admit, there was something adorably humorous about a peevish Kate.

"And you know, the worst part was that she ended up dumping him like, a month later, so we endured all that misery for nothing," she added.

"Wow. So you really do have a berserk button," Gail laughed.

"I've got a few. But that one is particularly sensitive."

"You sure you want to marry that?" Brink asked.

"Yeah, I'm pretty sure," Michael answered automatically. Then he physically felt his face fall.

"Pretty sure about what, Ghost Boy?" Gail asked.

"Uh..."

Lie! Lie! Hurry! his brain yelled at him. Unfortunately, lying on the spot was not his forte. Especially when he had not one but two exceptionally beautiful women waiting for an answer and an obnoxious teenage ghost guffawing in his ear.

"That... that production was even worse than the movie."

"Nice cover. Way to go," Brink grinned.

"Oh, it *was*. At least when I watched the movie, I got to look at Hugh Jackman," Kate griped. "But you know what? That's all I'm going to say about it. We are standing on one of the most famous shorelines in the world, about to sleep out under the stars in a place that is literally a fairy tale storybook come to life. And I want to enjoy every moment. Brink, that means no more talking."

"Until later, you know, when we're trying to prove to Caleb that you're real," Gail said.

"Do you really like him?" Kate asked. "I'm sorry. I'm so curious."

"I don't know him well enough to know if I like him. But he's... I don't know... sort of intriguing to me. And, like Mr. Hugh Jackman, he's fun to look at," Gail winked. "I'm also eager to see if we really can change his mind. I've never really understood the skeptical brain. I mean, even if I didn't believe in ghosts, I think I'd always be looking for a reason to believe in them, you know? Like Michael talks about in his book, I'd want that reassurance that life continues after death."

"You read my book?" Michael asked. He was pleasantly surprised. And honored. He didn't know Gail nearly as well as he did Luke. He'd always thought she was too cool for him.

"I did. I thought it was excellent. Very well-written. Way better than Luke's book."

Now Michael was definitely blushing.

"I don't know about that. But thank you."

"Oh, trust me. Luke is one of my best friends, but he's not a writer," Gail said. "He's more of an in-front-of-the-camera talent than a behind-the-keyboard one."

"I liked his book. But then, I'm really not much of a critic," Kate said.

"Unless it's a shitty production of *Les Mis*," Brink quipped.

"Of course, I like Michael's better, but I'm a little biased," Kate continued.

"Just a little," Gail grinned. Then she glanced over her shoulder to where Luke and the rest of the guys were throwing seasoned vegetables on their portable grill. Michael had to hand it to Luke; he really had thought of everything. "I'm going to go see if the guys need any help. Or, you know, if Caleb wants to sneak off and make out."

As soon as she was gone, Kate looked up at Michael, her eyes sparkling in the sunlight. Once again, Michael's thoughts drifted to the diamond ring in his suitcase. Was tonight the night? It *was* a really beautiful setting. And everyone was in a good mood for once.

Oh, God. It was really going to happen.

Suddenly, Michael couldn't feel his hands.

"Kate, I..." he began, but the words died in his throat.

"Wait a minute, is this it? Are you asking her?" Brink gasped.

Michael closed his eyes and tried to ignore him.

"Everything okay?" Kate asked, stroking his cheek.

Michael opened his eyes again.

"Yeah. You're just... You look so beautiful. I mean, you're *always* beautiful. But right here, right now... I'm kind of having a hard time believing you're real."

Kate just smiled. Then, as if to convince him, she ran her fingers through his hair and pulled him down into a long kiss. As he breathed in the sweet gardenia scent of her hair and savored the taste of her mouth on his, he realized that no matter how long they both lived, it wouldn't be long enough. He would always want this, always want her, always want more.

"Oi! Lakeside lovers!" Luke called out. Michael and Kate broke apart and blushed. "I hate to interrupt the snog-fest, but dinner is almost ready!"

"Do we really have to share a tent with him?" Michael muttered.

Kate, of course, just laughed.

The sun had yet to set by the time everyone had cleared their plates and cleaned up the campsite. Kate was surprised. She'd been certain that it would at least be dusk by the time they began their search for Nessie.

"What time is it?" she asked.

"Almost eight," Luke answered.

"Are you serious?" Kate wrinkled her nose and turned her gaze toward the bright sky.

"According to my weather app, the sun won't set here in the Highlands until 10:05 tonight," Peter announced.

"It was like that in Edinburgh, too. We were just too preoccupied to notice," J.T. reminded them.

"So we have two good hours of daylight to try to lure Nessie out of the murky depths. Perfect!" Luke exclaimed. "Let's get rolling!"

Within minutes, Peter and J.T. had their cameras in hand and Luke had taken his place at the edge of the lake, arms outstretched, ready to begin his introductory soliloquy.

"I'm standing here on the shoreline of one of the most mythical and most mysterious bodies of water on Earth. Nearly eight-hundred feet deep and twenty-three miles long, it is the largest volume of freshwater in Great Britain and home to one of the most famous legendary creatures of all time. Welcome... to Loch Ness."

"What, is he auditioning for a high school production of *Hamlet*?" Kate overheard Hayes mutter to someone behind her. Probably Gail. She seemed to be the closest thing to a friend that he had on this particular trip.

To her surprise, however, it wasn't Gail's voice that answered.

It was Michael's.

"Since we're in Scotland, it'd probably be *Macbeth*."

"Ah. Good point."

Kate whirled around to see Hayes and Michael standing side by side, watching Luke with the same bemused expression.

Wait, what?!

She knew she was gawking, but she couldn't help it. It was the absolute last thing that she expected to see. It would have made more sense to see Nessie herself crawl right up out of the loch, wearing a tam o'shanter and singing "God Save the Queen."

Meanwhile, Luke carried on with his introduction.

"We've all seen the famous photograph of a dino-like leviathan, raising its head up above the waters. Even though this particular photograph was snapped in 1934 by a London physician passing through the area, reports of a Loch Ness monster actually date back all the way to 500 A.D. Saint Columba, an Irish priest, is said to have blessed the loch and banished the beast in the year 565. But through the centuries, sightings persisted."

Interesting though the history of Nessie may have been, Kate found herself far more fascinated by the bizarre comradeship that seemed to be forming between Michael and the man who'd admitted to being out to destroy him.

"So wait, are you two friends now?" she asked.

"No," Michael answered.

"Absolutely not," Hayes agreed.

"When did this happen?" she asked.

"It didn't," Hayes insisted. "It just happens that your boyfriend, by some odd twist of fate, is the most normal member of this entourage."

"Really?" Michael asked.

"Oh my God, you just made his whole day," Kate told Hayes.

"Don't misunderstand me. I said he was the *most* normal. Considering our present company, that isn't saying a lot." Hayes cast a sideways glance toward Luke and the crew.

"So I'm gonna go out on a limb here and guess that you don't believe in Nessie either?" Kate asked.

"I'm going to go out on a similar limb and guess that you do?"

"I believe in ghosts more."

"How do you quantify belief? You either believe in something or you don't."

Kate hated to admit it, but it was a valid argument.

"I guess it's more that I like to believe that Nessie's out there. I can't say I know for certain one way or another, but I'm definitely open to the idea. With ghosts, however, I know for sure."

"How?"

It was a simple question, and a surprisingly sincere one at that. Kate only wished she knew how to answer. Where would she even begin?

She could tell him about Trevor, who'd haunted Gavin to the point of ailment and exhaustion. How, if it hadn't been for his very real presence in their lives, she would never have known that he'd existed. That she'd known him. That she'd loved him.

Then there was her experience with Sterling Hall, the man whose love for his wife, Joanna, had bound him to the mansion that he'd built for her for over a hundred years. His desperation to find his long-lost love had driven him to act

113

out. He eventually resorted to possessing Kate in order to force Michael to assist him in his search for Joanna.

And what about Brink? Brink had been a part of her life as long as Michael. He made his presence known so often and in so many ways that Kate barely spared a second thought over the fact that she couldn't see him. He was just as real to her as any of her other friends. Maybe even more so considering how often he interrupted her date nights with Michael.

And then, there was her own personal experience with the afterlife.

"I don't know how much you know about Michael and me personally," she finally began.

"Not a lot," Hayes admitted.

"About a year and a half ago, I was in a really bad car accident. I suffered a traumatic brain injury and I actually flatlined for about seven minutes."

"And you floated up into the clouds and looked down at your body in the ambulance. Am I right?"

"No. I was in an ambulance, thank God, otherwise I might not be standing here today. But I didn't float or see myself or anything like that. I actually ended up in a Starbucks."

"A Starbucks?" Hayes did not sound impressed.

"I know, not the ghost story you were expecting. But in spite of the cozy atmosphere, it was honestly one the scariest moments of my entire life. Or afterlife, I guess I should say."

"And why's that?"

"No one knew I was there. I was crying. I was screaming. It was like being inside a nightmare. No. It was like I didn't exist at all."

"So, what makes you so sure that this was real? That it wasn't just a hallucination?"

"Because that's when I first met Michael," Kate answered. "He saw me. He looked right at me and asked if I was all right. I didn't have time to answer. When we reconnected a few months later, I knew I knew him from somewhere, but I couldn't place him."

Hayes crossed his arms but said nothing.

"You don't believe a word of that, do you?" Michael asked him.

"No. It makes for a nice story, though."

"Well, at least you're not being a jerk about it. I'll call that a step in the right direction," Kate commented.

"I've told you before. I'm not a bad guy," Hayes said.

Kate, not at all convinced, simply shrugged in response.

"You don't believe that, do you?" Hayes pressed. Now he was smirking.

"Let's just say I'm skeptical," Kate finally answered.

And then, with an uncharacteristically flippant toss of her hair, she turned her attention back to Luke, the crew, and the sparkling, sun-kissed horizon of Loch Ness.

CHAPTER FIFTEEN

Two hours later, dusk had fallen. Stars glittered to life through billowy gray clouds and while the water still reflected the fading colors of the evening sky, the surrounding hills were already shrouded in darkness.

But there was still no sign of Nessie.

Of course, that hadn't dampened Luke's spirits in the slightest.

"I think it's time to build a campfire," he announced.

"I think it's time to sleep," Michael countered, stifling a huge yawn.

"Nonsense, Mikey! The night is still young! Besides, we need you to help us communicate with Brink!" Luke reminded him.

"You really don't. He will literally talk to anybody," Michael said.

"It's true. I will," Brink acknowledged.

"He agrees."

"Except clowns. I don't like clowns," Brink added.

Michael pressed a hand to his forehead and sighed.

"Come on, you don't want to miss out on the campfire. We'll have a few drinks, tell a few ghost stories. We might even make Scottish s'mores," Luke said as though he really thought that would be the clincher. Michael still wasn't convinced. "Dude, you really want to leave Kate all alone out here with us? And Hayes?"

That did it.

"Okay," he agreed.

"So," Luke dropped his voice so that no one else could overhear. "Have you given any thought as to where or when you're going to pop the question?"

"I've considered it half a dozen times already," Michael admitted.

"Well, just remember I want to be there to film it!"

"I remember," Michael promised.

"Good. Now let's go build a campfire!"

It didn't take long for J.T. and Peter to get a fire started, nor did it take the girls very long to change into their pajamas and gather up the shortbread, chocolate, and marshmallows for Scottish s'mores.

"You look so cozy," Michael smiled, taking a seat next to Kate.

She responded by wrapping her arms around his slender torso and snuggling up against him. Then she lifted her head up and kissed his neck. Michael felt his blood rush. Suddenly, he was wide awake.

"Okay, I think we're about ready!" Luke exclaimed, emerging from their shared tent with his new camera.

"We're filming this?" Peter asked through a mouthful of s'more.

"Of course," Luke said.

"I thought Caleb didn't want to be on the show," Gail said.

"Caleb *doesn't* want to be on the show," Hayes stated.

"Better to film it and not be able to use it than to have the skeptic become a believer and decide that he does want to be on the show after all and then not have the footage," Luke argued. "Now, who wants to hold the Ovilus?"

"I will. I don't want to hold a camera," J.T. admitted, reaching out for the device.

"I was going to set up a tripod anyway," Luke told him. "You think I'm missing out on s'mores?"

"You know, I wasn't sure about this shortbread, but it's actually not too bad," Peter remarked, helping himself to a second marshmallow.

"So Mikey, is Brink still around?" Luke asked.

"Yeah, he's here," Michael answered.

"Tell him I want a s'more," Brink said.

"Great! Okay, Brink, I think you're pretty familiar with all of our equipment. We have the Ovilus, the digital recorder, the EMF meter, which measures electromagnetic frequencies, and just for you, the swanky SB11 Spirit Box," Luke grinned, proudly displaying all of his ghost-hunting gadgets and gizmos.

"Cool." Brink seemed mildly impressed, but Michael knew his best friend well enough to know that he was still thinking about s'mores.

"Now then, before we officially begin, Mikey, why don't you tell us a little about Brink?" Luke asked.

Upon Luke's request, Brink's eyes lit up. Of course he was interested *now*.

"Yes, Michael, why don't you tell them the story of young Eugene John Brinkley? Born to Mark and Helen Brinkley in 1975, he was named for his grandfather who - "

"What would you like to know? Because he's about to rattle off his entire autobiography in my ear," Michael cut in.

"Well, for starters, how did you meet?" Luke asked.

"Ooh! Ooh! Let me answer this one!" Brink exclaimed.

"Fine," Michael sighed.

"Tell them that I was just going about my business, haunting my former teachers and watching out for my little sister, when I caught this gawky freshman with a weird-shaped head staring at me. Now this kid, I just knew was going to grow up to be a huge loser - "

"Why would I tell them that?"

" - in an endearing sort of way," Brink continued. "That's why I decided to take him under my wing."

"We met in high school," Michael translated.

"Man, you suck at this," Brink declared.

"And, forgive me if this is too personal, but how did he die?" Luke asked.

"Can you at least tell them it was something sort of badass?" Brink requested. "Like maybe something you'd see on *Game of Thrones*."

"**Thrones**," the Ovilus spoke.

"'Thrones?'" Once again, Hayes was not impressed.

"It was a skateboarding accident," Michael answered.

"So how did the robot box come up with 'thrones?'"

"He wanted me to tell you it was something cool, like on *Game of Thrones*," Michael explained.

"God, what a great show," Gail sighed.

"Will you ask Gail if she wants to be my girlfriend?" Brink asked.

"**Girlfriend**," the Ovilus echoed.

"Girlfriend?" Gail asked, glancing at the Ovilus with a flirtatious smirk. "Are you asking me out, Brink?"

"Yes."

"**Yes**."

"Ha! There! Did you hear that?" Luke exclaimed, pointing at the Ovilus. "That is an intelligent response!"

"That is a pre-programmed response," Hayes argued.

"Why don't we try the Spirit Box?" Peter suggested. "As cool as we all know the Ovilus is, I just don't think it's going to convince him."

"You might have a point there, Pete," Luke said. "Let's set up the Spirit Box."

"And what is this contraption supposed to do?" Hayes asked.

"That's an excellent question. The SB11, or the Spirit Box, scans radio waves and emits a sort of static, and we can actually hear spirits speak through that static," Luke answered. "Oh, and word of warning, it's a little irritating."

"As opposed to...?"

"Okay, I set myself up for that one," Luke remarked. "Here we go!"

Luke flipped the switch on the new device and immediately, the sound of slow, rhythmic static filled the night air.

"Ugh, that noise is awful," Brink griped.

"Noise... awful," his voice broke through the Spirit Box.

"Yeah, I know. But we can hear you! How cool is that?" Luke asked. "Do you want to answer some questions for us?"

"Okay," Brink agreed.

"...kay."

"Excellent. And just remember, you can use my energy if you need to. I would tell you to use Mikey's, but it's past his bedtime and he's running on fumes," Luke said.

"Thanks," Michael muttered, too tired to think of a snappy comeback.

"Okay, Brink, let's just start with a few easy questions. Can you tell me your full name?"

"Eugene John Brinkley."

"Eug...John Brinkley."

"Where are we right now?"

"Scotland. Loch Ness."

"Scotland... Ness."

"How long have you - "

"Stop." Hayes stood abruptly, cutting Luke off mid-question. "Please. Just stop."

"Why?" Luke asked. "We're getting genuine, intelligent answers here."

"You're getting broken snippets of rogue radio frequencies. And that *thing* is giving me a headache."

"That *thing* is allowing us to have a conversation with a man whose voice hasn't been heard in over twenty years!"

"Seriously, Luke, just give it a rest." This time it wasn't Hayes, or even Michael who spoke. It was Gail.

"What? Why?"

"Because we've had a great day and I don't want to see it end with another argument that neither of you will win," Gail said.

"So, you're saying you think we should give up?" Luke asked.

"No, I'm saying that I'd rather curl up in a blanket and enjoy the campfire than listen to the two of you bicker. Come on, tell me honestly, is this really how either of you wants to spend your evening?" Neither Luke nor Hayes answered her. "If the two of you just sat down, had a s'more, and tried talking about something *other* than what you don't agree on, I don't know, maybe you'll find you have something in common."

Luke crossed his arms over his chest and shook his head. Nevertheless, he turned to look at Hayes and for half a second, Michael truly thought they were about to have a civil conversation.

"Look. You're not an idiot. You know why I don't like you," Luke said. "To tell you the truth, I don't care what you believe. It's really never bothered me that you're a skeptic. But when you write those nasty articles and accuse me of preying on my fans' fears and emotions, it gets personal. *That's* when I start to have a problem.

"If you can't handle a little criticism, maybe you shouldn't be in the public eye," Hayes retaliated.

"I can handle criticism. What I don't appreciate are full-blown attacks on my character."

"Listen Rainer, do you want honesty? When I first began writing those articles, I had *no idea* they'd even reach you."

"Oh, yeah right."

"Why would I have any reason to think they would? You're *Luke Rainer*. You've got your celebrity status and legions of loyal followers. I'd have had to have been delusional to think that what I wrote would ever get back to you. Or that you'd actually take the time out of your schedule to respond to it," Hayes reasoned. "But then you started lashing out at me and I realized I'd triggered some kind of nerve."

"Yeah, you triggered a nerve!"

"But why? I'm a nameless professor from a small town in Oregon. I am literally the last person who should be any sort of threat to you. But the way you reacted... You'd have thought I'd just unearthed an actual human skeleton from your closet."

"I *told* you you should have just ignored him!" Kate exclaimed, pointing at Luke.

"*I* told him he should have just ignored him! At least a dozen times!" J.T. added.

"You do tend to get a little defensive from time to time, bro," Peter said. "Not to say that isn't part of your charm, but I can see how it might make some people think that you're a little insecure."

Luke didn't seem to know how to process all of the insights his friends were throwing at him. Michael had to admit he was right there with him. In the year that he'd really known Luke (and in the years he'd spent trying not to know him), he'd never once thought of his friend as any sort of insecure. If anything, Luke always presented as just the opposite. Confident. Cocky. One hundred percent sure of himself and what he believed in.

Yet there, beneath the vast Highland skies, Michael watched as an unfamiliar shadow of doubt crossed Luke's face.

But why?

He was *Luke Rainer*, as Hayes had so astutely pointed out. He was famous, well-traveled, filthy rich... How was there any room for doubt when he was a self-made success?

Michael didn't get the opportunity to ask.

"Well, you know, it's getting late," Luke announced, his forced tone a far cry from its usual vigor. "We should probably call it a night."

"Are you okay, Luke?" Gail asked.

"Of course. Why wouldn't I be?" Luke answered lightly. "I'm off to bed. Goodnight."

And then he disappeared into their tent, leaving a cold and awkward silence in his wake.

While the rest of the crew set about packing things up and extinguishing the fire, Michael noticed Kate's gaze drifting back to the tent.

"I've never seen him like that before," she murmured to Michael.

"Me neither," Michael said.

"Do you want to go check on him?" Kate asked.

"I don't know. He might not want to talk."

"But you might be able to help him feel better."

Michael sighed. Kate had always had so much more faith in him than he had in himself. Nevertheless, he *was* concerned about Luke. So while the crew carried on outside, Michael slipped away and followed Luke into the tent.

"Luke?"

"Hey, Mikey." Luke was already sprawled out on top of his sleeping bag, staring up at the tent's surprisingly sturdy ceiling.

"Are you okay? I know you told Gail you were okay, but Kate was worried..."

"Oh yeah, I'm fine. Just feeling a little pensive. And, you know, didn't really feel like helping clean up."

Michael nodded, but he knew that wasn't the whole story.

"Well, if you want to talk about anything... we're both here for you."

"I know," Luke sighed. "I just never like to think of myself as someone who needs someone to talk to. It makes me feel... weak."

"It doesn't make you weak. It makes you human," Michael reasoned. "Whatever you're feeling now, there's no shame in it.

"That's just the thing, though. There's a lot of shame."

"What? How?"

"Because... I'm wondering if maybe Hayes is right about me."

"You're kidding." Michael knew he sounded insensitive, but Luke wasn't making any sense.

"You see? This is why I don't talk about my feelings."

"I'm sorry. I'm sorry. Please, go on. Just... maybe explain the whole Hayes being right thing."

"I've believed in the paranormal since before I really understood what the paranormal was. I was six years old, playing in the living room, minding my own business when my grandpa walked in. I hadn't seen him in over a year, but I knew him immediately. The apparition looked like him, walked like him... it even smelled like him; like cherry tobacco and old books.

"Ever since that afternoon, I've been hell-bent on proving that what I saw was real. That I wasn't just some dumb kid with an overactive imagination. I believed so much that it used to physically pain me whenever someone would try to argue that ghosts didn't exist. So I started lashing out. Just like I did with Hayes."

"But that doesn't mean he's right about you. I think all that means is you shouldn't care so much about what other people think." That was quite possibly the most hypocritical piece of advice that Michael had ever had the audacity to offer anyone. But this wasn't about him. It was about Luke.

"Perhaps. But as Pete pointed out, I come off as insecure. And even though I've never thought of myself that way, maybe, deep down, I am. I mean, no matter how much I see, no matter how much I experience, there's always going to be that lingering 'what if...?' What if that noise really was just the building settling? What if that shadow figure really was just a shadow? What if..." Luke took a deep breath and closed his eyes. "What if I really didn't see the ghost of my grandfather that day?"

124

For a moment, Michael was too stunned to form a coherent thought. This was the very last conversation he'd ever expected to have with Luke. Luke! The guy who lived and breathed for the paranormal. The guy whose enthusiasm for the afterlife had skyrocketed him to world fame and fortune. Michael never would have imagined that he harbored even the slightest inkling of doubt.

"Luke, I can't tell you if you really saw him or if your six-year-old eyes saw what they wanted to see. But I can promise you – no – I can *swear* to you that you're not wrong. Even if he wasn't there that day, he *is* there. Maybe not somewhere where you or I can reach him. But he *is* there. They all are," Michael assured him. "I don't know if I ever told you this, but after my brother took his own life, I never saw his ghost. And that scared the living daylights out of me."

"No, you never told me," Luke said.

"I finally realized it was because he had moved on. His spirit had no reason to linger. But that's when I really began to understand that I only see the souls who are still here in this world. I have no idea what happens to the ones who've moved on. I don't know where they are or if there's any way to reach them. Maybe that's something that none of us will know until we get there ourselves."

"I hate not knowing," Luke grumbled. "But thank you. You're a good friend, Mikey."

"So are you."

"Well, there's always room for improvement," Luke laughed.

Although there were times that Michael would agree there was an argument for that sentiment, for the moment, he was relieved that Luke was acting more like his old self. For all his chaotic energy and quirky eccentricities, Luke was the heart and soul of *Cemetery Tours*, the force that held each and every one of them together. It would be a tragedy to see him lose his spirit. Especially over the likes of Caleb Hayes.

CHAPTER SIXTEEN

It turned out that being lulled to sleep by the gentle lapping of waves on the shoreline and the whispering of Highland wind wasn't quite the whimsical experience that Kate had been anticipating. In fact, it was actually sort of miserable.

She'd settled into the tent fully expecting a night of coziness and comfort in the company of her friends and the love of her life. Instead, she found herself wide awake until the odd hours of the early morning, tossing and turning and chilled to the bone on the hard, frigid ground. Of course, it only added insult to injury that her companions slept contentedly all night, with Michael snoring in one ear and Luke snoring in the other.

Next time, she was totally renting a pod.

Yet even after such a lousy night, it was hard to be cross with Michael waking up next to her, his eyes still heavy, his hair adorably tousled.

"Good morning," he greeted her.

She groaned pitifully in response.

"Oh? Not a good morning?" Michael asked.

"Didn't sleep well," she explained.

"Really? I slept great."

"I know," she glared playfully at him.

Outside, Luke and Peter were busy making breakfast for everyone while Gail, J.T., and Hayes struck the first tent. While Michael volunteered to help take down the second, Kate made a beeline for the steaming pot of freshly brewed coffee.

"Need a little pick-me-up, Beautiful?" Luke grinned.

"Just a little," Kate answered.

"Did the kelpies keep you up?"

"The what?"

"Shape-shifting water spirits. Didn't you study up on your Scottish folklore at all?"

"Luke. I love you. But it is too early for this conversation."

"Nonsense! It's never too early to talk kelpies."

And even though Kate still had no idea what he was talking about, she laughed. Sleep deprivation aside, she was happy to see Luke smiling. It seemed that last night's episode with Hayes hadn't affected him in the slightest.

After breakfast, Bill arrived to pick them up. Although Kate was more than eager to bid their campsite farewell, she couldn't resist taking one last look back at the loch. Maybe it was her imagination, or the fact that she was running on about thirty minutes of sleep, but she could have sworn she caught a glimpse of a creature with a long, graceful neck diving down into the depths as the morning sunlight sparkled on the surface of the water.

"So, who wants to know where we're going today?" Luke asked once they hit the open road.

"Where are we going today, Luke?" Peter asked.

"I'm glad you asked, Pete. Today, we are continuing on our quest to document the most enchanted parts of Scotland before settling in for our stay in a centuries-old haunted castle. Our first stop is the Isle of Skye, home to fairies, giants, and an entity known as a glaistig. Our final destination, however, is Dunadhar Castle."

"That name is familiar to me," Kate commented, resting her head on Michael's shoulder.

"It's actually not one of Scotland's better-known castles. In fact, it was only recently restored, I think for another television show," Luke told her.

"It was *The Queen's Surrogate*," Gail supplied.

"Oh my God, I love that book," Kate gasped. It was honestly the trashiest thing she'd ever read, but she'd finished it, plus it's three equally trashy follow-up novels, in less than a week.

"I've never heard of it in my life," Luke quipped.

"Not true! I caught you reading my copy during that godawful layover in Pittsburgh!" Gail exclaimed. "And don't even try to deny it because I posted it to my Snapchat story!"

"She did. I still have the screenshot saved to my phone," Kate said.

"So do I," J.T. quipped.

"You know, the history of Dunadhar Castle isn't exactly a love story," Luke interjected loudly, effectively ending the trashy romance conversation. "Like most of the castles, it's seen its fair share of bloodshed and heartache. Several spirits are said to haunt the grounds, but the most famous is the ghost of Flora Colville. I will tell you more of her tragic tale tonight."

"You sound like an infomercial," Hayes remarked.

"Why Caleb, that's the nicest thing you've said to me all week."

It was a three-hour drive to the Isle of Skye, and although Kate didn't want to miss a moment, she caught herself drifting in and out of sleep early on in the journey. At one point, she felt Michael take her hand, his lithe fingers toying gently with hers. In that moment, everything was right in the world.

But then... just as she drifted off, a memory fought its way to the forefront of her mind. She was sitting on a couch, watching a movie. It was a movie she'd seen before, but that didn't matter. All that mattered was the hand holding hers, the warmth of his breath on her cheek, the promise of the diamond ring glittering on her finger...

Trevor.

Kate gasped, startling Michael as much as herself.

"Are you okay?" he asked her.

"Yeah," she answered, taking a deep breath. "Yeah, I'm fine."

And she was. She really was fine. At least, she thought she was. And even if she wasn't, there was no need to say anything to Michael. After all, she couldn't be certain that what she'd just experienced was even a real memory. It may have just been a dream, a vivid hallucination brought on by exhaustion or perhaps the familiarity of Michael's touch.

But it had seemed so *real*. She could still feel Trevor's body next to hers. She could still smell his cologne.

Oh God... she trembled.

It wasn't real. It couldn't be real. If it was real, that would mean she was beginning to remember. And she didn't want to remember. She had grieved for Trevor, for the love that they'd shared, and for the future they'd lost, but it hadn't been the same grief that she knew she would have experienced had she truly remembered their time together. In a strange way, the memory loss that she'd suffered had spared her heart. If those memories were to suddenly come flooding back... she would be broken.

It's okay. You're okay. You're in Scotland, remember? You're on an adventure. You're living in a fairy tale. You're with Michael.

Michael...

What would become of him if she recovered those lost memories? He wouldn't leave her. She was sure of that. They'd been through too much together. They loved each other too much. But she knew that her grief would have a devastating impact on him. Her broken heart would shatter his as well. She didn't want to do that to him. Hurting him in any way was unfathomable.

Forget. Just forget, she told herself over and over again. *Don't dwell. Don't despair. Just forget.*

So she turned her attention to the majestic mountains outside her window. She wondered what the world might be like atop those heights, those vast, rolling hills. She imagined feeling the wind in her hair, the kiss of the sky on her face. Scotland had already made it easy for her to believe in magic, but the Highlands made it easy to believe she may very well learn to fly.

Michael couldn't shake the feeling that something was off.

Kate was happy. She was smiling. Her eyes sparkled as she gazed at the clear turquoise waters and delicate falls of the Fairy Pools. But there was *something*.

When he'd asked her if there was anything bothering her, she'd claimed that she was just tired. That may have been the case. Part of it, anyway. He remembered her telling him that she hadn't slept well. Perhaps trying to stay alert had thrown off her energy.

But what if there *was* something else? What if she was feeling ill? Or homesick? What if something Hayes had said had resonated with her the same way it had Luke? Whatever it was, Michael found himself unable to concentrate on anything Luke told them about Green Ladies or hobgoblins or any of the other fairy tale creatures that supposedly roamed the Isle of Skye.

And of course, Kate noticed.

"What's wrong?" she asked, linking her arm through his. "You seem so distracted."

"Sorry," he grinned sheepishly.

"Are you still worried about me?"

"Yeah."

"Please, don't be. I promise you I'm fine. I had a weird dream on the bus and it... confused me for a little while. But everything is wonderful."

"You would tell me if it wasn't though, wouldn't you? You know you can tell me anything."

"I would. And I know. And I love you for it." To prove it, she rose up on her tip-toes and pressed her lips gently to his. "Now promise me that you'll stop worrying. It's far too beautiful out here to waste a single moment dwelling on doubt. Don't forget we're chasing fairies." She winked and flashed him her brightest smile.

Michael smiled, too. It was hard to argue with her, especially when she looked at him like that, with true love and unadulterated joy. She was right. He wanted to enjoy his time with her chasing fairies around the Isle of Skye. Because he knew, sooner rather than later, they would be back to chasing ghosts.

"Dunadhar Castle has stood, guarding the hills of the Highlands, since the early fourteenth century. This ancient fortress has seen war and famine. It has housed royalty, priests, and prisoners. Today, it is a popular tourist destination, preserved and protected by the Scottish Historical Society. But it is also protected by the ghosts who have called this castle home for nearly four-hundred years." Luke paused. Then he looked back at Peter. "How was that? Was that good?"

"I think you said it all," Pete told him.

"I don't know. I think it felt a little choppy," Luke frowned.

"Oh my God, you can do a voiceover later," Gail moaned. "Come on. Callan's waiting for us."

"Don't worry about Callan. I'm sure Hayes is keeping him plenty entertained."

Callan McHale, the castle's curator, was a short, scholarly man with a headful of curly blond hair, perfectly round wire-rimmed glasses, and an almost childlike enthusiasm for history. Hayes, having finally met something of a kindred spirit, all but leapt at Callan's offer to show him the castle's catalog of ancient documents. While those two geeked out over land deeds, Luke and the crew decided to take advantage of the hazy daylight and shoot a brief introduction outside the castle.

Now, of course, Gail was getting antsy, J.T. and Pete were going to say whatever they thought that Luke wanted to hear, and Mikey and Kate had disengaged entirely. Mikey even had the audacity to be scrolling through his phone! And he *never* checked social media!

"Why don't we give it one more take? Then we can call it a wrap," Luke said.

"Okay, fine. *One* more," Gail agreed.

As far as Luke was concerned, filming a decent introduction was the hardest part of the job. Most of the sites they investigated were so rich with history and abundant in fascinating tales that it was impossible to do them justice with a thirty-second speech. Luke wanted his viewers to know everything. He wanted them to experience these places the way that he experienced them. But time was limited and he needed to save most of it for the actual investigations.

So his crew humored him while he made one last valiant effort to capture the essence of Dunadhar Castle. He still wasn't entirely satisfied, but then again, he rarely ever was.

Callan and Hayes were waiting for them in the entry hall, still pouring over ancient literature.

"... but what's really interesting is - oh, hello!" Callan greeted them with a cheerful smile. "Are you ready for your tour, then?"

"We are ready, Callan!" Luke told him.

Unlike the polished grandeur of Edinburgh Castle, the corridors of Dunadhar were as dark and cold as the stones that formed them. Still, there was an archaic elegance in their simplicity that Luke appreciated. He felt as though he'd truly taken a step back through time.

As they navigated the twists and turns, Callan told them every story he knew, pointing out exquisite tapestries, paintings, and shields and explaining the significance of the Colville clan crest.

"As you can see, the crest bears the image of a young hind, or a female deer. The deer represents peace, strength, and fortitude. But if you ask me, it's the clan's motto that really strikes a haunting chord, given the history. *Oblier Ne Puis*. It means 'I cannot forget.' And there's a lot that this castle hasn't forgotten."

"So you believe in ghosts, too?" Hayes sounded disappointed, like he'd lost his one and only ally.

"Oh, of course. You can't spend too much time in a place like this and not believe," Callan chuckled. Luke decided then that he liked Callan. He had a very jovial, very innocent air about him.

"Tell us about some of your experiences, Callan," Luke said.

"All right. Before I do, though, do you all know the story of Flora Colville?"

"I do. I haven't told the others yet," Luke answered.

"Then let me enlighten them. We have three known ghosts haunting this castle and several others who remain unknown. The three we've identified are a soldier, a midwife, and of course, young Lady Flora. She was the youngest child of Lord Eoin Colville and his wife, Lorna, and easily the most adored. Eoin and Lorna cherished her above all else, showering her with praise and affection and extravagant gifts. This, as you can imagine, made her older siblings bitterly jealous.

"Flora grew up to be a kind and exceptionally beautiful young woman, far lovelier than any of her sisters. And of course, they took notice. So they, along with their brothers, devised a wicked scheme. They went to their father, claiming they had seen Flora in the village, keeping company with an elderly woman, long-suspected of practicing witchcraft. Additionally, they collected plants and herbs and they even acquired a cauldron to plant in Flora's bedchamber.

"Eoin was devastated, but he wasn't about to see his precious daughter burned at the stake. So he kept her hidden, locked away, deep within the heart of the castle. Eventually, her isolation drove her to madness. She lost her ability to communicate, tore her hair out in clumps. She even attacked the maid assigned to her care, viciously scratching up her face like a rabid animal. She died only a few months later, a fortnight before her twenty-first birthday."

"God, that poor girl," Kate whimpered.

"It is a very sad tale, and one that has no ending. Flora is still here, trapped within the very walls she once called home," Callan said.

"You can't be serious," Hayes remarked.

"Oh, but I am," Callan insisted. "I know Flora exists just as surely as I know the sun will rise."

"How?" Hayes demanded.

Callan wasn't intimidated. He remained calm, collected, and confident as he looked Hayes straight in the eye and answered his question with unquestioning assurance.

"Because I've seen her."

CHAPTER SEVENTEEN

After their harrowing encounters with Bloody Mackenzie and Mr. Boots, Michael had been of the mindset that the ghosts of Dunadhar Castle would be delightful in comparison. But the longer he listened to Callan recount his experiences with Flora, the more he began to realize just how foolishly optimistic he had been in thinking so.

"She tends to appear more often when I'm alone, or with a very small crowd. I don't think she likes a lot of attention. She doesn't know what to make of it. I can't tell you for certain, but psychic mediums who have tried to communicate with her in the past claim that death did not grant her her sanity. She doesn't know she's dead. She barely even knows her own name."

"Well, you know, Mikey here is one of those mediums," Luke told Callan.

"Are you really?" Callan looked thrilled.

"I don't know if I'd call myself a medium - "

"How do you do it?" Callan asked, cutting him off. "Do you hear their voices in your head? Do you have to summon them? Or is it one of those instances where they speak through you?"

"Um... none of the above," he answered honestly, fully aware that that made him sound like the most disappointing medium ever. "They're just there. I see them. I hear them. Just like the living."

"Fascinating," Callan marveled. "I've met others who share connections with spirits, and those who claim to see them in different realms. But this is a first. Have you ever met anyone who shared your gift?"

"Yeah, I have, actually," Michael answered. "A teenage girl in Maine."

"Forgive me if I seem too inquisitive. I've always been very eager to learn more about what happens after we die. Being here with Flora... oh, she's changed my life. Taught me so much, given me so much hope. I've studied history all my life and I hated that every story of every remarkable person ended with death. What would they have thought if they'd been allowed to watch history unfold? You know, it's like reaching the end of your favorite novel, wondering what goes on in the lives of the characters outside the pages."

"There you have it. You just answered your own question," Hayes commented.

"I'm sorry?" Callan asked.

"You compared the deceased figures of history to characters in a storybook. What do they have in common?" Hayes waited a beat before he continued. "They don't *exist*. Not anymore, anyway. Their ideas, their legacies might live on. But just like your fictional characters, those great men and women of history are no more than words on a page."

"Quite the dreary outlook you've got," Callan commented.

"It's the truth. And in my experience, accepting the truth makes everything a lot less complicated. There's no doubt. No second-guessing."

"I understand what you're saying. I'm a scholar, too. It's in our nature to trust in what we can know and see and touch. But I was also taught to never stop asking questions. To never close my mind to any possibility."

"So tell us more about your encounters with Flora," Luke interjected before Hayes had the opportunity to rebut.

"Well, I wish I could say that she's a lovely girl and a joy to anyone who crosses her path, but the truth is she's quite a fright to behold. Scares me out of my wits every time I see her."

"I thought you said she changed your life," Peter remarked.

"And she did. She made me a believer," Callan professed. "But she's no beauty. If you see her face, you won't forget it. She'll haunt your dreams."

Oh great. That was *exactly* what Michael needed. It wasn't enough that he still saw Mr. Boots' milky eyes staring into nowhere or Bloody Mackenzie's grisly hands wrapping around Hayes' throat. Now he had another ghoulish ghost to add to the list.

"Is there any way I could convince you to blindfold me?" he muttered to Kate.

"Oh, I think there are a lot of ways you could convince me," she teased. Then she burst into a fit of giggles, probably because of the look on Michael's face. "I'm sorry, I'm sorry. I couldn't resist."

"I mean, not that I'm opposed..." Michael blushed.

"Oh, good. For a moment, I thought I'd scandalized you," she winked.

Meanwhile, Luke was asking, "So Callan, if you don't mind my asking, what *does* Flora look like?"

"Thin. Bone thin. With wiry blonde hair and eyes wide with horrors we could never even begin to fathom. She wears a single garment, dirty and ragged, and when she looks at you, she sort of tilts her head to the side, like she's trying to make sense of what she's seeing," Callan answered. "I feel for the lass. I really do. Neither life nor death has been kind to her."

"Well, maybe we can help. After all, that is what we do," Luke said.

Hayes scoffed. Luke ignored him.

For the next hour, Callan led them through every corridor, every chamber, and every tower of the castle. Michael tried his best to pay attention; to appreciate the details of each room and absorb all the information that Callan shared. But all the while, he kept an eye out for Flora. If she was there, he didn't want her to catch him off guard. He didn't want to upset her, either.

Thankfully, the only ghost to show up was Brink.

"Oh *man*, this castle is *cool*! This is exactly like being in *Game of Thrones*!" he exclaimed. "Have you seen any of the ghosts here yet? *Are* there any ghosts here? Because you know, if they really want this castle to be haunted, *I* could move in. Eugene Brinkley, the Ghost King of the Highlands!"

"Yeah, that's sure to catch on," Michael remarked.

"The best part is I'm already dead so no one can stab me at my wedding."

"*What?*"

But Brink didn't bother to explain, which Michael decided was fine. He probably didn't want to know, anyway.

After dinner at a quaint restaurant in neighboring Dornie and a quick detour to see Eilean Donan, they returned to Dunadhar Castle for the first of their two-night investigation.

"Okay, so this first night is just a normal night," Luke explained. "Well, normal as far as paranormal investigations go. We'll set up cameras, of course. Maybe conduct a quick séance by candlelight in the Great Hall. Then we go about our own business, sort of like we're staying in a really fancy hotel. But tomorrow night, get ready. Because we will be pulling out all the supernatural stops. Any questions?"

"Yeah, I've got one," Gail announced, raising her hand. "What's the shower situation here? Because I slept outside last night. And there is definitely no shower in my bathroom."

"This is a seven-hundred-year-old castle. Be thankful you have a toilet," Peter teased.

Gail glared daggers in response.

"Yeah, so. Hygiene." Luke cleared his throat and Michael got the distinct impression that he had been hoping to avoid this conversation. "The good news is that there is a bathroom with a functional bathtub. The bad news is it's the only one."

"Are you kidding?" Kate looked alarmed.

"Don't worry. We can all use it. It just... might take a while," Luke grinned sheepishly. "The ladies, of course, are welcome to go first."

"Thank you," Gail huffed. "Kate, go for it."

"No, no. You go ahead," Kate answered. "I kind of want to go up and get settled into our room."

"That's fine," Luke said. "We'll begin our séance in about an hour if you and Mikey would like to join us. If not, you kids have a fun night."

"Do séances actually work?" Brink wondered aloud as he followed Michael and Kate up the narrow, winding staircase leading to their bedchamber.

"I hope not," Michael muttered. Kate glanced up at him with curious eyes. "Brink wants to know if séances work."

"Oh." Kate nodded. "Do you not want to go? We don't have to."

"I don't mind if we go. I just don't want it to work," Michael answered.

"Yeah, but do you ever?" Brink asked.

Kate, however, seemed to understand.

"The energy here is definitely... different. Not necessarily in a bad way," she observed. "It's almost uncertain. Like, I can't fully trust it. But it isn't malicious."

"Are you sure you're not just sensing Brink?" Michael asked.

"Rude," Brink declared.

"Trust me, I know Brink's energy. His is cool and light, like a spring breeze. The energy here is heavier. Ancient. It's like the castle itself is alive with memories and it's longing to make those memories known."

"That's like what Callan said," Michael suddenly recalled. "'There's a lot that this castle hasn't forgotten.'"

Without warning, Kate's face paled and again, Michael sensed that something was troubling her. "Hey, what's wrong? Are you okay?"

"Yeah. Yeah, I'm okay."

"Are you feeling sick?"

"No. Just... a bit of a headache," she answered. "I'm fine. I promise."

Their conversation carried them all the way to their bedchamber: a cozy room in one of the towers with a small fireplace, a four-poster bed with crimson-colored curtains, and windows facing the forested mountains surrounding the castle.

"Maybe we should go to bed early. Call it a night," Michael suggested.

"No way. We're in a haunted castle. I'm not missing out on anything."

"But if you're not feeling well - "

"You know you're beginning to sound like me, right?" Kate teased him. "I think I just need a good night's sleep."

"Then let's skip the séance," Michael pleaded with her. "We can enjoy an evening together, just the two of us. We've been so distracted, so busy with ghosts and graveyards, that even though I've been with you almost every moment, I feel like I haven't spent very much time with you at all. And... I miss you."

Kate took a deep breath and Michael realized with a start that she was trying not to cry. Before he could reach out to comfort her, however, she'd wrapped her arms around his neck and pressed her lips to his with such force, she nearly knocked him off his feet. Ordinarily, Michael would never question such a kiss, but something about the way she clung to him concerned him. It was like she was trying to convince herself that he was real.

But then, she broke away from him and wiped her tear-stained cheeks with her sleeve.

"Okay," she whispered. "We'll stay."

Nothing extraordinary happened in those precious few hours, but Michael knew that when he looked back on their first night in Dunadhar castle, he would remember it as one of the best nights of his entire life.

First, he lit a fire while Kate selected a soft acoustic playlist from her Spotify app. Then, she rummaged through her backpack until she found her dilapidated copy of *The Princess Bride*, which they had been reading together ever since Michael confessed to her that he'd never read it. Finally, they gathered all the pillows and blankets from the bed and arranged them in front of the fireplace.

Michael wrapped a soft, wool blanket around their shoulders as Kate draped her legs over his and settled into his arms. Once they were comfortable, she turned to the page in the book where they'd left off.

"You know what's really cool?" she asked.

"What's that?"

"We're reading *The Princess Bride* in a real castle."

"Too bad we don't have a TV in here. We could watch the movie."

"You're not allowed to watch it until after we've finished the book."

"I thought that was the *Harry Potter* rule."

"It applies to every literary classic," she answered with a grin.

They took turns reading up until the chapter titled The Wedding. By then, the fire had dimmed to embers and both Michael and Kate were fading fast. It wasn't until Kate turned and snuggled up against him, however, that Michael finally whispered, "Do you want to go get into bed?"

She answered with a sleepy nod.

Carrying their pillows and blankets, they climbed in through the curtains and nestled themselves into each other's arms for the night. Michael knew Kate would be asleep within seconds, but he fought to stay awake a few moments longer, just so he could make it all last. Her warmth. Her breath. Her touch.

What he wouldn't give for a thousand nights just like this one.

What he wouldn't give for only one.

CHAPTER EIGHTEEN

Michael's mind was still heavy with sleep when he stirred a few hours later.

At least, it may have been hours. It may have been mere minutes. For all he knew, two days could have passed since he'd fallen asleep next to Kate in their Highland castle tower. It was simply too dark to tell.

Sleep. Back to sleep, his body commanded. And Michael was only too happy to obey.

Then he heard it.

It was so soft that he first thought he'd imagined it. But then it came again. A whimper. A wail. Echoing in the dead of night.

Someone was crying.

Alarmed, he immediately thought of Kate, but she still slept peacefully beside him. The mournful sobs hadn't disturbed her in the slightest. Michael didn't have to wonder why.

Frightened, confused, and utterly conflicted, he closed his eyes and silently prayed that the spirit's weeping would cease, that she would somehow find the comfort she so desperately sought without him or anyone else being forced to intervene. Instead, her anguished cries grew steadily louder as she drew ever closer, finally passing by right outside their chamber door. Michael shuddered as he listened to her faint footsteps fading into the darkness.

Gone. She's gone. It's over.

But her voice soon returned, sniffling and speaking in broken phrases.

"Red as scarlet. White as snow. Go ye cursed. Go ye cursed. He is come out of his place. Go ye cursed. Go ye cursed. Go ye cursed. Into the fire everlasting. Red as scarlet. *White as snow...*"

It almost sounded like a poem. A chant.

Or an incantation.

Michael's blood froze in his veins. Flora Colville was a witch. That was why she'd been imprisoned in her own home: so that her family could contain her.

No. No, it was an accusation. A false accusation, he told himself. He was being irrational, letting his anxiety get the better of him. Flora wasn't a witch. Clearly, he was so tired that he wasn't thinking straight.

But his hazy reasoning brought him no solace. If anything, it reminded him that Flora Colville was, in all likelihood, an innocent girl, betrayed and locked away by her own family. Her older siblings were supposed to love and protect her, yet they'd been the ones to strike her down.

Slowly but surely, Michael's apprehension began to waiver, and before he could change his mind, he climbed out of bed and crept onto the landing outside their room. Flora was nowhere to be seen, but he could hear her. She'd moved further away, down a few stories, her whimpers drifting up into the cool, empty tower.

Steadying himself in the dizzying darkness, Michael pressed his hand against the stones lining the wall and carefully made his way down the winding staircase. It was unsettlingly quiet inside the castle and he didn't want to wake anyone.

He followed Flora's voice to the ground floor and into an open room, dimly lit by a pool of moonlight pouring in through the windows. As his eyes adjusted, the furnishings inside began to take shape. Soon, Michael could clearly make out a magnificent fireplace, an antique reading bench, and shelves and shelves and shelves of books. The library.

Although there was no sign of Flora, Michael quickly sensed that he wasn't alone. Sure enough, a subtle movement out of the corner of his eye directed his attention to a tall, shadow figure standing in front of one of the bookshelves. Not at all convinced that his would be a welcome presence, Michael hastily stumbled back out of the room. But in doing so, he tripped and toppled over a small antique table.

The figure swore and whirled around.

"*Sinclair*! What the *hell* are you doing?"

Hayes.

"I thought - I mean - What are *you* doing?" Oh yeah, that was eloquent.

"I'm in a library. What do you think I'm doing?"

"But why are you down here in the dark? Why don't you have a flashlight or something?"

"I could ask you the same question, but since you failed to answer my first, I don't really see the point."

"I thought I heard something," Michael explained.

"You did. It was me."

"No. I..." Michael stopped himself. He could describe every step that had led him from his lofty bedchamber to the library, but what was the point? Hayes wouldn't believe him. He didn't want to believe. "Never mind."

But Hayes knew what he was going to say.

"You thought you heard a ghost?"

Before Michael could muster up a response, however, a heavy object toppled off one of the shelves and hit the floor with a loud *thud*. Both men whirled around to see a book lying on the ground amidst a cloud of settling dust.

While Hayes muttered something about not setting it back on the shelf properly, Michael's eyes scanned the room once more. Flora was there. She had to be.

And suddenly, she was.

Huddled in the corner of the library, halfway concealed by her own silvery blonde hair, the ghost grasped at the wall while she whispered her incoherent poetry over and over.

She wore a simple white nightdress as Callan had described, and she appeared frail and sickly, almost gaunt. She was also, for the moment, totally oblivious to their presence.

"Thou wilt not despise. Spare us. Be clean. Let our cry come unto thee. Broken and contrite. Broken and contrite."

As he listened to her utter the same phrase over and over, Michael realized that it wasn't a poem or an incantation at all. It was a prayer.

"Sinclair!" Hayes hissed, snapping Michael out of his stupor.

"Sorry," Michael muttered.

"Maybe you should go back to bed."

"Maybe you're right," Michael agreed. And yet, he remained firmly planted where he stood. Now that he'd found Flora, he couldn't bring himself to let her out of his sight. *Had she cast a spell on him?* Or was it pity that held him in his place? He couldn't be sure. Either way, he wasn't about to leave her.

Hayes began to grow agitated.

"You know, that wasn't so much a suggestion as a subtle hint," he said.

"I know."

"So, why are you still here?"

Michael didn't answer. Instead, he took two cautious steps toward the spirit.

"Flora?" he gently called her name.

She moaned in response, but she didn't look at him.

"Flora?" Hayes asked. "The mad girl?"

But Michael continued to ignore him as he approached Flora, still visibly distraught.

"Let our cry come unto thee. Let our cry come unto thee..." she whispered.

"Flora?" He was close enough now that, had she been alive, he could have reached out and touched her. "Flora."

With a sharp gasp, finally, she turned to face him. Staring into her eyes, those wide, tortured eyes, Michael

146

fought every urge to turn away. It wasn't the sight of her that unnerved him. It was the way she looked at him with a sort of feral ferocity; her head tilted, her brows furrowed, her shoulders hunched. It was like she was preparing to defend herself.

Like she thought he was dangerous.

"It's okay," he continued hastily. "My name is Michael. I... I want to help you."

Flora exhaled through gritted teeth and muttered something under her breath.

"I'm sorry?" Michael asked. "I didn't... didn't quite catch that."

"*Witch*," she hissed.

"Witch?" Michael asked. "No, you're not. I know you're not. You're just - "

"*Witch*," she said again. "Witch. Witch." She repeated it over and over, her pale blue eyes glowing fiercely in the moonlight. It was only then that Michael realized that her cries weren't a confession. They were an accusation. "Witch. *Witch. WITCH!*"

Michael tried to back away, but it was too late. With a shrill, earsplitting shriek, Flora lunged forward, arms outstretched. She hit Michael with a rush of cold air, an electric shock of vertigo, and one brief burst of disorientation before everything went black.

When he opened his eyes again, he was lying on an unfamiliar couch, gazing up at the firelight flickering in Kate's concerned hazel eyes.

"Hey," she greeted him with a warm smile. "Are you okay?"

"I think so," he answered tentatively. "What... what happened?"

"Well, Hayes seems to think you have some kind of weird food poisoning, but I'm willing to bet this has more to

147

do with spirits than salmonella," Luke answered with a typical Luke response.

"You fainted in the library. Hayes came to get us. Then he and Luke moved you into the drawing room," Kate told him. "You gave him a bit of a scare, you know. He kept asking if you had any medicine that you could take or if we needed to call a doctor back home."

"He was concerned about me?" Michael found that hard to believe.

"Well, all things considered, he'd have to be a psychopath to not be at least a *little* concerned," Luke said. "I mean, according to him, you dropped like a dead fly. Hell, I think for half a second, he thought you *were* dead."

"I guess I should probably thank him," Michael murmured.

"There's no need," Hayes announced, appearing in the doorway. "I did what anyone would have done."

"Still. I appreciate it," Michael told him.

"Well, you're welcome," Hayes said. "But I've got to tell you, Sinclair, after what I saw tonight, I'd strongly suggest you seek professional help."

For once, his words weren't callous or malicious. He spoke with absolute sincerity. Michael couldn't decide if that made an already humiliating situation better or worse.

"Thanks, Caleb. I'll... consider it," he said.

"Good," Hayes said. "Now get some rest."

And with that, he left the room.

"You know, sometimes he almost seems human," Luke remarked lightly.

"He's trying," Kate said. "He is completely out of his element, here."

Luke gave a reluctant nod of acknowledgment before changing the subject.

"So Mikey, what was she like?" he asked.

"Who?"

"'Who?' Flora! You saw her, right?"

148

"Oh. Right," Michael replied, pressing a palm to his aching forehead and squeezing his eyes shut. "She was exactly what Callan said she would be."

"So he's got the gift too?" Luke asked.

"No. I think she's just powerful. Lost, confused, angry. And she's been alone for a long time."

"Well, hopefully she won't take her angst out on you tomorrow night," Luke commented.

"Oh, I really don't think she wants to see me again," Michael said. And if he was being honest, he wasn't wild about the idea of seeing her again, either.

"Why not?"

"I think she's scared of me."

"Scared of *you*?" Luke snickered. Rather loudly. Far more loudly than Michael thought was really necessary. "I'm sorry, I'm sorry. But why would she be scared of you? Look at you. You're about as terrifying as a Disney Princess."

Michael sighed.

"I think she thinks I'm... a witch."

"Huh. So I actually wasn't too far off the mark," Luke said.

"Ha ha."

"Seriously, Mikey, it does sort of make sense. You're probably the first person to look her in the eye in centuries. The first person to speak directly to her instead of around her. Even in her state of mind, she's got to know that you can't be, well, normal."

"And after what she went through, it's no surprise that she'd be terrified of anyone she thought might be a witch," Kate surmised.

"So does this mean that I'm excused from the hunt tomorrow night?" Michael asked.

"If you don't already know the answer to that question, you are the worst psychic ever," Luke responded.

Oh, well. It was worth a shot.

CHAPTER NINETEEN

Luke didn't know if it was something in the water or if the moon had slipped into some strange phase in the sky, but everyone, *everyone* was in a mood and for the life of him, he couldn't figure out why.

Okay, he knew why Mikey was acting sort of off. He hadn't slept well. He'd had his lights punched out by a ghost. He had every right and reason to not be one hundred percent himself.

Kate was a similar story. She was worried about Mikey, so naturally, she'd be a little distant and distracted.

Hayes' lousy attitude was easily explainable because, well, he *was* a lousy attitude.

Everyone else, though? They had no excuse.

But Luke was nothing if not a team player. If his crew needed a day off to decompress and recharge, then that's what they were going to get.

"Okay, compadres. Listen up!" he exclaimed, addressing the group as they sat down to a breakfast of leftover oatmeal and day-old fruit. Okay, so maybe the lackluster energy made a little sense. "It has come to my attention that the morale around leaves a lot to be desired. Ergo, I am declaring today a holiday."

"Ergo?" Gail raised an eyebrow.

Luke ignored her.

"Until eight o'clock this evening, you are free to do what you want. You can sleep. You can explore the castle. You can even go into town. But tonight, I want everyone to bring their ghost-hunting A game. I'm talking high spirits, positive energy, and enough enthusiasm to put your high school pep squad to shame. Does that sound fair?" His friends voiced their agreement. "Good. Now that that's settled, I think I'll go for a morning hike. Would anyone care to join me?"

"You mean you haven't had enough nature after the lake and the camping and the gallivanting around the Isle of Skye looking for Frodo and Orlando Bloom?" Gail asked.

"Okay, so that's a no from Gail."

"I'll go!" Kate announced.

"Excellent," Luke grinned. He knew he could count on her. "Mikey? You in?"

Of course, he already knew the answer to that. If Kate was going, Mikey would undoubtedly tag along.

"Yeah, sure," he answered.

"Great! Anyone else?" Luke asked. He was met with a deafening silence. "Fair enough."

While Mikey and Kate retreated back to their room to change, Luke threw together a backpack of outdoor essentials: water bottle, video camera, portable phone charger, potato crisps, and a waterproof jacket just in case it started to rain. So far, Scotland had blessed them with mostly clear skies, but Luke figured it was better to be safe than soggy.

"So why are we doing this?" Mikey asked once Luke joined him and Kate in the entrance hall.

"What? Taking a day off? I'm not a tyrant, Mikey," Luke responded, leading the way out of the castle and into the dense forest of pine surrounding it.

"No, I get that. I mean why are we going on a hike?"

"Do we need a reason? We're in the Highlands! I want to take in the glory of an ancient wilderness."

"So, we're not running off to find some weird druid burial ground? We're really just... going out for a hike?"

"We're really just going for a hike," Luke swore. "Unless, of course, you *know* of a druid burial ground. Then, by all means, lead the way!"

"That would be pretty cool," Kate grinned.

"No, no. Definitely not cool," Mikey insisted.

Kate just laughed.

"So, Mikey, are you feeling better?" Luke asked.

"Yeah, I am. Could have used a few hours of extra sleep."

"You can always take a nap when we get back," Kate told him.

"I'd actually recommend that since we're going to have a late night tonight," Luke said.

"You still think that's a good idea?" Mikey asked.

"Have I ever *not* had a good idea?" Luke countered.

"How about inviting Caleb Hayes along?" Mikey replied.

"Or picking fights on social media?" Kate added.

"Provoking Sterling Hall?"

"Breaking into the bridal barn."

"That whole mess with Chance McDermott..."

"Wow, you two have a real knack for making lists," Luke cut in. "Not that I agree with the subject matter. But really, it's impressive."

"Sorry, we'll stop," Kate giggled.

"No, no, keep it up. Just maybe make it something more along the lines of why Luke is the best. Or why everyone should watch *Cemetery Tours*."

"Seems like you're well on your way to making your own list," Mikey commented.

"Kate, tell me, is he this much of a smart-ass when it's just you two? Because I feel like that level of snark has the potential to be a real mood-killer," Luke said.

"He... has a very dry sense of humor," Kate replied. "Most of the time, I find it charming."

"Hold on to her, Mikey," Luke advised.

Kate beamed at Mikey, and as usual, he melted on the spot.

Then again, that may have been perspiration. Mikey wasn't exactly a shining example of athleticism. The poor kid was so tall and scrawny. Really, it was no wonder Flora had been able to wipe him out with a single blow.

"You know, I really am glad that we did this," Kate said. "It's nice to just get to hang out with you guys."

"It is," Luke agreed. "And listen, I know that this trip isn't turning out how you'd probably thought it would, but I hope you're both still happy that you came."

"Oh, I am," Kate said. "I mean, I've seen castles and mountains, lochs and fairy pools... Everything about Scotland is just... magic."

"Even with the ghosts?" Luke grinned.

"Well, we knew what we were getting into," Kate said.

"I could do without the ghosts," Mikey remarked.

"We know. But you're always such a good sport about it," Luke grinned.

They followed the forested pathway to a small but open clearing, its perimeter marked only by a barbed iron fence.

"Looks like we've reached the edge of the property," Kate said. "I guess we should turn a - "

"Wait a minute, what are those?" Mikey interrupted.

"What?"

"Those!"

Luke and Kate followed his gaze to three brown, shaggy-haired bovines grazing at the far end of the field.

"A-ha! *Those* are the reason we're here, Mikey!" Luke announced. "Say hello to the heeland coos!"

"The heeland who?" Mikey asked.

"Highland cows! Affectionately known as heeland coos! I wanted to see one so much the last time I was here and somehow, never managed to find one. But then Bill told me about this little family that lived just on the other side of the hiking trail and I knew I just had to see them!"

"So, in other words, you *did* have an ulterior motive in getting us out here." Mikey crossed his arms like he was gearing up for a lecture, but even he couldn't keep the smile off of his face. Especially when the little calf toddled over to greet them.

"Okay, maybe I did," Luke admitted. "But I *really* didn't think I'd get anyone to come with me if I said I wanted to run off to a stranger's pasture to look at some cows."

"No, you definitely wouldn't have."

"I still would have come. Just look at her!" Kate knelt down to get a better look at the calf. "Oh, you are just precious, aren't you? Yes, you are..."

"So uh..." Luke pulled Mikey aside while Kate fawned over the baby coo. "Have any idea about when you might... you know... put a ring on it?"

"Not yet," Mikey sighed.

"Dude. We've already been here four days. We've only got four days left. You'd better get a move on it."

"I know, I know. I've just... been a little distracted."

"Yeah, I get that. It has been sort of crazy, hasn't it? But you know if you need anything at all, all you have to do is ask."

"Thanks, Luke. Really. I appreciate it."

"Any time, Mikey. Any time."

Kate was still smiling by the time they returned to Dunadhar Castle. A morning hike with Michael and Luke had been just what she'd needed to uplift and refresh her spirits.

However, it had also left her feeling grimy and gross. She needed a bath. Desperately.

So while Michael climbed back into bed to rest, Kate gathered up her toiletries, a towel, and her comfiest pair of yoga pants and began her trek downstairs, praying the entire way that the only bathroom with a working tub would be empty.

She'd only just reached the ground floor, however, when a tall figure turned a sharp corner into the stairwell, colliding with Kate in the process.

"Oof!" the figure huffed as Kate's shampoo and hairbrush tumbled to the ground.

"I'm sorry," Kate apologized automatically.

"No, no. It was my fault," Hayes insisted, kneeling down to help Kate collect her things.

"Thanks."

"Actually, Kate, I'm glad to have run into you. Not literally, of course. But I have been hoping to speak with you."

"Me? Why?"

"Would you care to go somewhere a little more private?"

"No, here's fine," Kate answered firmly. She had no idea what he could possibly have to say to her, but she did know that she didn't care to be alone with him under any circumstances.

"Very well," Hayes agreed. "I just wanted you to know that I meant what I said last night. I'm concerned about Michael. I think his... condition... is far more serious than he realizes. Than any of you realize."

"Look, I know this is coming from a good place. In fact, I think it's nice that you're so worried about him - "

"You mean to tell me that you're not?" Hayes asked her. "After all you've witnessed in just the last four days? You're not worried about him at all?"

"Of course I worry about him. I worry about him all the time."

"And yet you've never advised him to get some help?"

"It's not exactly something you can prescribe away."

"I'm not even saying he needs medication. Just... someone to talk to. To help him work through his issues - "

"He doesn't *have* any issues." Now Kate was beginning to feel defensive. "He's just trying to figure out how to play the hand he was dealt. The same as all of us."

"No, Kate," Hayes insisted. "I know you want to believe that. And he puts on a very convincing act, I'll give him that. But if you really cared about him, you wouldn't enable him. You would encourage him to accept reality - "

"He does accept - "

" - and the reality is - "

"I already know how you feel - "

" - there are no such things as ghosts."

Kate sighed. It was a conversation that could be had a thousand times over and it would still lead to nowhere. She would never be able to convince him that life didn't end with death, just as he would never change her mind about Michael. She knew him. She knew his heart and soul. And she knew his gift was real. It was frustrating when others couldn't see it, didn't even try to understand it, but in the end, it didn't matter. She would stand by and support Michael no matter what.

But she was also done arguing. It was nothing but a waste of time and energy. And she was definitely feeling drained.

"Okay, fine. I get it," she sighed. "Now, may I please go take a bath?" *I need to wash off your scathing condescension.*

"Be my guest." Hayes stepped aside. "Thank you, Kate."

Kate didn't respond. The last thing she wanted from Caleb Hayes was gratitude. Especially when he was only thanking her because he believed he'd won his war.

CHAPTER TWENTY

Michael had fallen asleep to a stream of sunlight shining in through his tower window, but when he woke a few hours later, angry storm clouds were rolling in and the Highland wind was howling through the castle turrets. It would have been the perfect setting for another night spent reading with Kate by the fireplace.

If only it weren't for the ghost.

Reaching up to rub the sleep from his eyes, Michael was seriously considering lying back down when he realized that he wasn't alone in bed. Kate slept silently next to him, her lips parted slightly, her blonde hair fluttering as she breathed. The sight of her was enough to make Michael's heart skip a beat and any apprehension that he may have felt instantly evaporated. It was remarkable, the effect her presence had on him.

She stirred a few moments later, stretching and sighing before finally gazing up at him with sleepy, starry eyes.

"Hi," Michael greeted her.

"Hi," she smiled. "You look like you feel better."

"I do," he told her. "I think this was just what I needed."

"I'm glad," she said. Then, she took his face in her hands and gently pulled him down into a kiss.

"This is how it was supposed to be," Michael murmured, not fully aware of what he was saying or even thinking.

"What do you mean?" Kate asked.

"This trip. Scotland. Us," Michael answered. "Just you and me. It should have been just you and me."

"It's just you and me now," Kate reminded him.

She was right. They were together. They were alone. In a castle in the Highlands at the edge of a thunderstorm. It was everything he hadn't dreamed to hope for.

Marry me. Kate, will you marry me? The words echoed inside his mind as they had so many times before. And yet, like so many times before, he found himself holding his tongue. *Not yet. Not yet.*

But if not now, when?

"Kate," he whispered. "I..."

"Yes?" The way she looked at him, her hazel eyes soft with adoration, made Michael wonder if she could hear the unspoken words as he recited them over and over again in his thoughts. Did she know? Did she suspect? Was she secretly hoping?

But once again, words seemed to fail him. So instead of speaking, he lowered himself back down and pressed his lips to hers.

"This is how I want to spend the rest of my life," she sighed, lacing her fingers through his. "With you, exploring far-off lands, having adventures with baby coos..."

"And no ghosts," Michael added.

"I don't mind the ghosts. As long as they respect you. And don't try to hurt you."

"You really wouldn't prefer to just have a normal life? A normal boyfriend?"

"I really wouldn't, and do you know why? Because my life would have been haunted either way. And if you had been like everybody else, you might not have been able to help me. You may not have even believed me," she reasoned. "Our lives would be very different if you were just another 'normal' guy."

"I guess we wouldn't be here, would we?" Michael asked.

"Definitely not," Kate said. "We wouldn't have been to Maine or to Hugo. We wouldn't have been able to help Gavin or Trevor. We definitely wouldn't know Luke. And don't you dare say that may have been for the better!"

"Wha - ? I wasn't going to!" Michael insisted.

"Maybe not, but you were thinking it," Kate accused playfully.

"How do you know?"

"I can read your mind."

"Oh, really?" Michael laughed.

"Yeah. I'm a psychic, too."

"In that case, what am I thinking now?"

"Oh, that's easy," Kate smiled. "You're thinking you want to kiss me again."

And she was absolutely right.

By the time they finally climbed out of bed, the sky had opened up and a steady rain was falling outside the castle walls. While Michael pulled a plaid flannel shirt on up over his shoulders, Kate changed into leggings, an oversized sweatshirt, and her comfiest pair of boots. It wasn't exactly your typical ghost-hunting attire, but she felt oddly at home there inside Dunadhar Castle.

Just as the clock prepared to strike eight, they left the cozy confines of their bedchamber and made the descent down to the ground floor. The rest of the crew, including Hayes, had already reconvened and were waiting in the great hall.

"Ah, Mikey, Kate. How nice of you to be almost punctual," Luke commented.

"What? It's only - " Michael paused to check the time on his watch. "7:56. We're four minutes early."

"Four minutes early is eleven minutes late in the paranormal business. The film business too, for that matter," Luke told them.

"Then why didn't you tell us to meet you at 7:45?" Michael asked.

"I'd hoped you would know better, Mikey."

Michael winced and rubbed his forehead while Kate tried not to laugh.

The investigation began in the library. As per Luke's instructions, every lamp had been turned off and every candle extinguished, so the dull glow of the brewing thunderstorm became their only source of light.

"Okay, I'm going to do a quick intro, and then Mikey, I want you to tell the viewers, in your own words, about your encounter with Flora. Sound good?" Luke asked.

"Sure, Luke."

"Living for that enthusiasm, Mikey. Now, come stand over here. Actually - no, wait. Go and stand over where you saw her and we'll bring the cameras to you."

While Luke and the crew went about setting the scene, Kate turned her eyes toward the rows and rows of dusty old books. Their titles were faded and their covers were frayed, but there was something breathtakingly beautiful about the collection of ancient literature. Beautiful and yet so strangely familiar.

"I want a library just like this one."

Kate felt her breath catch in her throat. She'd spoken those words. The memory was clear as day. And then...

Oh, God...

He was there. In memories so vivid she could feel his strong arms slip around her waist as he leaned forward to kiss the top of her head. She remembered glancing around, smiling up at him, taking in his handsome features.

"One day, I'll build you as many bookshelves as you want," he'd promised her.

"But will they be in a castle?" she'd teased.

"I might have to wait a few years before I'm able to work a castle into my budget..."

In the memory, she'd laughed. He'd loved to make her laugh. And oh, how easily he'd been able to do so. In reality, however, her heart ached so deeply, so desperately, that she

160

felt a physical pain in her chest. She clasped her hand over her mouth to keep from crying out.

Forget. Forget. Please, forget, she prayed as frantic tears began to stream down her cheeks.

But try as she might to erase all traces of Trevor from her mind, he remained. Everything she'd loved about him in that brief moment was suddenly engraved forever in the forefront of her memory. His warm eyes. His open heart. His carefree laugh. His vibrant spirit.

He was real. And he was so *alive*. It was impossible to imagine otherwise.

He's not gone. He can't be gone.

"Kate?" She heard Michael call her name. He sounded alarmed. "Kate! What's the matter? What's wrong?"

"Nothing, I'm fine," Kate insisted, feigning nonchalance. But she overplayed it, and the second she looked into Michael's wide, frightened eyes, she collapsed, weeping, into his arms.

"Please. Please, tell me," Michael begged.

"I... I don't know," she sobbed. She knew that he deserved the truth, but her broken heart wouldn't permit her to speak.

"It's Flora," Luke deduced.

"What?" Michael asked.

"Last night, you said that she was distraught, right? What if this is her energy influencing Kate?" Luke asked. "Kate, how are you feeling? Do you feel like there's someone with you?"

No. This wasn't Flora. This was her own haunted spirit, her own crushing grief. But Luke had provided her with an explanation that wasn't the truth, and for that, she was grateful.

"I feel... sad and... and confused," she whimpered. "I'm sorry..."

"No, don't apologize," Michael told her. "Maybe we should stop this, Luke."

"But if Flora is trying to communicate with us through Kate, don't you think we should listen to what she has to say?" Luke asked.

"Not if she's going to hurt her!"

"She's not hurting her. Kate's just... really sensitive," Luke tried to argue, but Kate could hear the hesitation in his voice.

"Or maybe she's just had enough," Hayes commented.

"Oh, don't you start," Luke warned.

"What? I can't be concerned about her?"

"Enough!" Kate cried. "Please, just stop."

And just like that, the bickering ended and a heavy silence descended upon the library. Kate took several deep breaths and fought to regain her composure. Her memory of Trevor still lingered, like a jagged dagger inside of her heart, but it was just that: a single memory. She should take solace in the fact that, for the most part, he was still a stranger, a second-hand story of what had once been love. And yet that single memory had invoked an emotional response so powerful it had all but rendered her helpless.

What would become of her if all their moments together returned? How could she endure that kind of anguish?

Then, just like an answer to an unspoken prayer, Michael leaned down and pressed his lips to the top of her head, just as Trevor had done in her memory.

Michael.

"You're okay," he whispered. "I promise. Everything will be okay."

And despite every ounce of fear and loss and uncertainty inside of her heart, she believed him. He was her strength, her comfort. He was the reason that she would make it through whatever hardships or heartaches lay ahead.

She only hoped that she wouldn't break his heart along the way.

Although Luke remained convinced that Kate's breakdown had been a product of Flora's negative energy, Michael wasn't so easily sold. It was true that Kate was often able to sense a spirit's presence, but he'd never known one to wreak such havoc on her emotions. Or anyone's, for that matter.

"What if Kate's more than just a sensitive? What if she's an empath?" Luke argued.

"A what?" Michael asked.

"Someone who feels what others are feeling. In other words, if there's a spirit around and she's projecting a lot of sadness and confusion, Kate would be able to feel that."

"So, why hasn't this happened before?"

"Maybe it has and we just didn't realize it. Or maybe those other ghosts weren't as powerful as Flora," Luke said. "Kate, *has* this ever happened before?"

"I don't think so," Kate answered listlessly.

Her sadness cut through Michael like a knife. He couldn't bear to see her this way. Just hours earlier, she had been so happy, so full of hope and wonder and love. Now, it was as though every ounce of who she was had drained away, leaving a wilted flower in her place. Was it an effect of the undeniably powerful energy within the walls of Dunadhar Castle? Or was it something else entirely? Michael needed to know. He loved Kate too much to let her suffer alone.

"Tell me what you need," he begged her as Luke and the rest of the crew migrated out into the corridor. "Tell me what I can do."

"There's nothing," she whispered without meeting his gaze. "I'll be okay."

It was in that moment that Michael knew something was wrong. Very wrong. Kate was an open book. She told him everything, often more than he could possibly need to know. It was one of her quirks, but it was also something that he loved and admired about her.

Before he could press her further, however, she slipped her arms around his waist and rested her head against his chest. Her embrace didn't relieve Michael of all of his anxiety, but it did bring him a few blessed moments of peace. Even if she wasn't ready to speak, she knew that she could still turn to him for comfort, for love, and for protection. And that meant more than words could ever hope to say.

CHAPTER TWENTY-ONE

By the next morning, the storm clouds had lifted and the sun once again smiled down on them as they traveled south to the seaside town of Oban.

"We're not actually staying in Oban," Luke clarified. "We're catching the ferry there that will transport us to the Isle of Mull. From there, we'll take a second ferry to Iona, an island shrouded in myth and mystery, a landing place of saints and Vikings, and a resting place of kings."

"You know we're not filming now," Gail remarked.

"I know, I was just trying it out. Sounded pretty good, huh?"

Gail raised an eyebrow in response.

"What's really cool about Iona is that Macbeth is supposedly buried there," Peter said.

"Wait a minute. Macbeth was a real person?" Mikey asked, looking genuinely interested for what was probably the first time in his life.

"Macbeth was a real *king*," Luke corrected him.

"That is so cool!" Kate exclaimed. Luke was glad to see that she was back to her bright, cheerful self. He'd never admit it, but her sudden bout of sadness the night before had unnerved him. It had hit her with such severity that at first, Luke truly believed that she'd been possessed. Thankfully, that hadn't been the case, but Luke still suspected that a spirit was to blame.

If only they'd been able to prove it.

After Kate had pulled herself together, neither she nor Mikey had been in any sort of mood to carry on with the investigation. While Luke couldn't say he blamed them, he was also of the mindset that their absence had discouraged Flora from making any further contact. But he wasn't going to dwell on that. He could have. But he wasn't.

The truth was they had collected enough evidence in Edinburgh alone to make for a compelling Halloween special, but as always, Luke wanted more. He wanted paranormal proof so concrete that no one, not even Caleb Hayes, could question its authenticity. And he was hoping that the mystical Isle of Iona held the key.

"What are you working on?" Luke heard Gail ask.

He glanced over his shoulder to see Gail gazing at Hayes as he scribbled away in a tattered old notebook.

"Just taking some notes," Hayes responded.

"Better not be your next smear campaign," Luke muttered.

"If you must know, this has nothing to do with you," Hayes assured him.

"Oh. Good." That at least made Luke feel a little better.

"So tell me, Caleb, has there been anything about this trip that you've actually enjoyed?" Gail asked.

"It's had its moments," Hayes acknowledged.

"Such as...?"

"Getting to see a few of Scotland's most iconic landmarks. Learning more about its history."

"What about us?" Gail pressed.

Hayes thought for a moment.

"I never fully appreciated how dedicated you are to your research. I'll admit that I'm impressed by how much time and energy you spend really getting to know a place and it's supposed ghosts."

"But you're still not a believer, are you?"

"No," Hayes answered. "I'm still not a believer."

"What do you think it would take?" Gail asked.

"I'd say a miracle, but - "

"But you don't believe in those, either."

Hayes shook his head.

"Well, maybe Iona will change your mind," Luke said. "Because you know, it isn't just a royal burial ground. It's known around the world as Saint Columba's Sacred Isle, one of the holiest sites on Earth, and a thin veil between the realms. It's the perfect place for miracles, whether you believe in them or not."

Kate breathed in the salty sea breeze and smiled. After a long and sorrowful night, fighting back memories and tears, she found happiness in the open air of the Highlands, comfort in the colors of Oban, and peace in the promise of Iona. Even though Trevor was still very much on the forefront of her mind, the ache in her heart had dulled enough for her to live once again in the moment. And this particular moment was one of sea spray, distant mountains, and misty lighthouses as the Caledonian MacBrayne Ferry chartered them across sparkling waters to the Isle of Mull.

"What? No," Michael said, out of the blue. "Yes, I'm sure."

"Of what?" Kate asked.

"Brink wants to know if he can get seasick... You don't have a working stomach. How could you possibly be nauseous?... Yeah, okay, but *The Sixth Sense* is a movie," Michael argued. Kate raised a confused eyebrow. "Apparently there's a ghost that throws up in *The Sixth Sense*?"

"Oh, right. I remember her," Kate grimaced.

"No, that does not prove your point," Michael told Brink. "... I don't think ectoplasm is even real."

It was too much. Kate couldn't help but laugh at the absurdity of their conversation. And that was only what she could hear of it.

She was so preoccupied listening to Michael banter back and forth with Brink that she didn't realize Hayes had joined them on deck until he cleared his throat.

"Oh, it's you," Kate remarked, fully aware of how rude she sounded.

"Sorry to disappoint you," Hayes quipped. "I'm glad to see you're feeling better."

"Thank you," she replied, desperately wishing he hadn't broached the subject of the night before.

"Listen, I know you still don't fully trust me, but I just wanted to tell you that if you ever need to talk about anything, anything at all, I'm available," he said.

"That's uncharacteristically generous of you," she commented.

"Be that as it may, I actually am a very good listener. And who knows? I might even be able to help you."

"Wait a minute." Kate narrowed her eyes. "Are you seriously suggesting you act as my therapist?"

"Of course not. Not formally, anyway. But after seeing you break down the way you did last night, I have to admit that I'm worried about you, too. Even more so than I am about Michael. And that... is saying something," he added, casting a sideways glance toward Michael, still engaged in a spirited conversation with his invisible best friend.

"Gee, how chivalrous."

"I know you don't want to hear this, and please don't take this the wrong way, but I think you being with him puts you under a lot of pressure. More than you probably realize. More than is good for you."

Before, Kate had only been mildly irritated with him. But those last words left her so stunned, so angry, that she felt her head begin to spin.

"Being with him is the best thing that ever happened to me," she insisted, far more forcefully than she intended. Her harsh tone alerted Michael to Hayes' presence.

"What's going on?" he asked, abandoning his debate with Brink.

"Nothing," Kate answered, all the while glaring at Hayes.

"I was just checking up on Kate. I wanted to make sure that our conversation yesterday hadn't upset her," Hayes answered.

"Wait, wait. What conversation?" Michael asked.

"You mean you didn't tell him?" Hayes asked Kate. "Why would you withhold something like that?"

"Because it wasn't worth mentioning," Kate snapped.

"What did he say? *Did* he upset you?" Michael asked.

"No, he didn't." And really, he hadn't. He had actually been rather easy to ignore. The first time, anyway. "He was just reiterating his concern for you. Come on," she said, taking Michael's hand. She'd had enough of Hayes, and she could tell by the expression on his face that Michael had as well. "Let's go get something to eat."

"Ugh, did she have to mention food?" Brink moaned, trudging along after Michael and Kate as they made their way into the ferry's concession stand.

"Okay, for the last time, you are not seasick," Michael muttered. And even if he was, there were more pressing matters at hand. "What was Hayes saying to you?" he asked Kate.

"Oh, you know. Just his usual nonsense," Kate answered.

There it was again. The aloof non-answer. Suddenly, Michael felt his stomach turning, too.

"Why don't you want to tell me?" Michael asked. "Are you afraid it's going to hurt me?"

"What? No. I just..." Kate trailed off and took a deep breath. "I don't want to dignify him, you know? Whatever he thinks is not worth my time or energy. And it's certainly not worth yours."

"But he's in your head. I saw it out there on the deck. And I know you're strong, but you shouldn't have to bear that burden alone. Please. Tell me."

Finally, finally, she met his eye.

"He thinks you're sick. He thinks that you need help. And he thinks that I'm losing my mind trying to keep up with all of it."

"All of what?"

"What he believes is some elaborate charade to keep convincing everyone that ghosts are real." She spoke as though the words had left a bitter taste in her mouth.

"He thinks I'm not good for you," Michael translated.

"Which is garbage. And that's exactly what I told him," Kate said.

"Don't do it," Brink warned.

"Do what?" Michael asked.

"Don't you dare start dwelling on what that ivy league dweeb says."

"I wasn't going to - "

"You were. I can see it in your face. Don't."

"Wasn't going to what?" Kate asked.

"Brink thinks I'm going to start worrying that - " But somehow, Michael couldn't bring himself to finish the sentence.

"That Hayes might be right?" Kate completed the thought for him. "He *isn't*. Not by any stretch of the imagination."

"But last night - "

"Last night had nothing to do with you or with him. It was... a weird moment. One that I doubt I would have been able to endure without you," she confessed, taking both of his hands. "I need you. You keep me safe. Never question it." Then, she rose up on her toes and kissed him lightly on the mouth. "Never doubt it."

"I won't," he whispered. It wasn't a promise that would be easy to keep, but it was one he knew he needed to make. Because, he realized, if he were to question or to doubt, he shouldn't be asking Kate to be his wife. He wanted her for better, for poorer, in sickness, and in health. But he also wanted to know that he was the man she deserved, the man who *would* keep her safe.

I am. I will.

"I love you," Kate said, her voice soft and gentle.

"I love you, too." If there was one thing on Earth that Michael could be sure of, it was that.

CHAPTER TWENTY-TWO

"Do you believe in Heaven?"

It was a question Michael had been asked on more than one occasion. It was also one of many that he'd never quite figured out how to answer.

In so many ways, it should have been an easy yes. After all, if he could proclaim with absolute certainty that ghosts existed, Heaven shouldn't have been much of a stretch. Especially when he'd borne witness to several spirits crossing over to the other side.

The problem was he couldn't say for sure what was on the other side.

Heaven could have been a golden city in the clouds, or perhaps a splendid banquet hall surrounded by dearly departed loved ones. Maybe it was a field of wildflowers on a summer's day or a shimmering kingdom of sapphire and starlight.

Or maybe, just maybe, it was the Isle of Iona.

It wasn't the hills just beyond the sparkling white sands or the colorful fishing boats floating in crystal clear turquoise waters. It wasn't even the elegant Abbey keeping watch over the coastline. No. It was something that couldn't be seen, touched, or even explained. It was something in the air that felt like magic, something in the water that felt like salvation.

Luke had described Iona as a "thin veil," a "sacred isle," but to Michael, it seemed to be so much more. With its astounding beauty and tranquil atmosphere, Michael wouldn't have been surprised to learn he was standing on Heaven's very shores.

"I didn't even know places like this existed," Kate sighed as a gentle sea breeze toyed with her long blonde hair. "I mean, of course I've seen pictures but... they really don't do it justice, do they?"

"Not even close," Michael agreed.

"Wow," Luke declared, joining them on the beach. "Can you feel that? This place is *teeming* with energy."

"I do feel it, but it's not a high energy," Kate observed. "It's more of a peaceful energy. Like it wants me to reflect... to be still."

"We can't be still. We have too much to do, starting with our tour of the Abbey in just over an hour, which just barely gives us enough time to drop our bags off at our hostel," Luke rambled.

"Wait," Michael cut in. "Why would it take us an hour to drop our bags off?"

He should have known better than to ask.

Iona, it turned out, had very strict rules and regulations concerning motorized vehicles. No cars were allowed on the island, just bikes and the occasional golf cart. The absence of auto fumes and screeching tires would have been quite refreshing... had their hostel not been located on the north side of the island, a two-mile hike from the ferry dock.

"Luke, this was a terrible idea," Gail grumbled about ten minutes into their journey.

"You'll change your mind once you see the hostel," Luke assured her.

"Yeah, that's another thing. Why are we staying in a hostel and not like... a bed and breakfast?"

"Because I want us to really experience everything that is Iona. The hostel here isn't like the ones in the big cities. It's like a home. We'll prepare our own meals, make our own beds... it's simplicity at its finest."

"That sounds like *housework* at its finest. Do I look like a domestic goddess to you?"

"I think it'll be great," Peter piped up. "I'm going to the market after our Abbey tour if anyone would like to join me."

"Count me in, brother," Luke said. "We can make up a list of anything anyone else needs once we reach the hostel. Sound good to everyone?"

"Sounds good," Kate said.

"Yeah... good..." Michael agreed, desperately trying not to sound as winded as he felt. He didn't need the entire group knowing just how out of shape he was.

Brink, of course, was all too eager to point it out.

"Dude, you look like you're about to keel over. And that's coming from a dead guy."

"Thanks," Michael huffed.

"Seriously, are you okay? When was the last time you did some cardio?"

"Do I... look like... I work out?"

"Maybe you need to start eating more protein. Or maybe, I don't know, look into getting an inhaler."

"Please stop... talking."

By what Michael could only describe as an act of God, he managed to keep up with the rest of the group until they reached the hostel. It was, as Luke described, a very quaint, home-like building with an entry hall, a kitchen, a reading nook, three bedrooms, and two bathrooms. What Luke hadn't happened to mention, however, was that it sat atop a lofty hill overlooking yet another perfect, secluded beach.

This is it, Michael thought to himself. This was everything he could have hoped for and more for Kate's proposal. Simple. Heavenly. Intimate.

This is it.

Or it would be soon. After his feet recovered from the two-mile trek. And definitely after he showered. And maybe after a quick nap -

"Okay, gang, time to head out!" Luke called.

"You have *got* to be kidding me," Michael deadpanned.

"Not even a little bit. Now, come on. Let's go."

"Where?"

"Already told you. Abbey tour. Supposed to be there in twenty-five minutes so we'd better hustle."

"But wait... isn't that... that's back where we came from!"

"I know, Mikey. That's why we need to go. Hurry up. Shake a leg."

"I can't even *move* my legs."

"Do you want me to give you a piggyback ride?"

"What? No!"

"Then quit complaining and get a move on."

With one last weary glance back at the bed he was leaving behind, Michael followed Luke and the rest of the group outside, to where Kate and Gail were already waiting and ready to go.

"Hey, there you are! Can you believe this view?" Kate asked him. "We've got to go exploring later. I bet we can climb down to the beach."

Great. More hiking. Of course for Kate, Michael would have crawled across a bed of burning coals. All she had to do was say the word and he'd follow her wherever she wanted to go.

The trek back to Iona Abbey, while not a walk in the clouds by any means, wasn't nearly as rough on Michael's legs or back as their initial journey to the hostel. Probably because they weren't hauling nearly two-weeks' worth of luggage this time around. It was also for that reason that Michael was finally able to really take in and appreciate the sights and sounds of life on the island.

Those sights and sounds, however, were not at all what he'd been expecting.

As it turned out, Iona was home to a lot of farm animals. To the right, a herd of goats. To the left, a herd of cows. And then there was a single, solitary rooster strolling casually down the same road they walked. Luke, of course, made a point to film it.

"Hey, look! We've made a friend!" he exclaimed, following the rooster with his phone.

"The first guest star on our spin-off series, *Cemetery Chickens*!" Peter laughed.

"*Paranormal Poultry*," J.T. supplied.

"*Haunted Hens*!" Luke added.

"Okay, boys, they get it," Gail cut in.

"Just one more! *Supernatural Nuggets*!" Peter declared.

"Oh, come on. That's just mean," Luke scolded.

Peter and Kate doubled up with laughter. J.T. snickered into his sleeve. Even Hayes cracked a smile.

Maybe Luke was right, Michael thought dryly. *Maybe Iona really is a place for miracles.*

Their tour guide was waiting for them when they arrived at the Abbey.

"There you are! Welcome!" she exclaimed with an eager smile. She was blonde and petite and couldn't have been older than twenty or so. "My name is Mollie and I'll be leading you on your tour today."

Luke stepped forward to shake her hand.

"Nice to meet you. I'm - "

"Luke Rainer! Trust me, I know. I'm a big fan."

"Well, thank you," Luke grinned.

"I don't share this very often, but I had a very difficult time coping with my Nan's passing. She raised me, you see. And after she died, I just felt lost. Alone. But you and your crew... you helped to remind me that she wasn't really gone. That she was still with me, and that I will see her again. And I... I've always wanted to thank you for that."

"No, Mollie. Thank *you*. Stories like yours are the reason we do what we do, and will continue to do what we do," Luke told her.

Michael could practically feel Hayes rolling his eyes, but thankfully, the skeptic remained silent.

"I'm glad to hear it," Mollie beamed. "Now then, before we begin, does anyone have any questions?"

"I've got one for you, Mollie," Peter spoke up. "Is this place haunted?"

"Yes."

"You sound certain."

"I am," Mollie told him. "Now, I can't speak from personal experience, but I have done my research and I can tell you, beyond the shadow of a doubt, the Isle of Iona is home to a number of restless spirits."

"That's what I like to hear," Luke grinned.

"It actually comes as a surprise to many that one of the world's most beautiful and sacred sites is also one of the most haunted. But there are a few very dark chapters in Iona's history. For example, did you happen to notice that strip of beach when you disembarked the ferry? That beach is known as Martyr's Bay, and it is named so for the sixty-eight monks who were slaughtered by Vikings that stormed the shore more than twelve-hundred years ago. Now what's interesting is that visitors will report seeing these ghostly monks... even though most of them have never heard the story."

"That's crazy," J.T. remarked.

"Yes, it's very sad," Mollie acknowledges. "But perhaps the saddest and strangest tale is that of Opal Murray, a young occultist who came to stay on Iona in the 1920s. Now, just as Iona has served as a holy destination for religious pilgrims, its reputation as a thin place draws in those who seek to practice magic and summon spirits."

As if on cue, all eyes turned to Luke. He shrugged.

"Guilty. Though I wouldn't go so far as to call myself an occultist."

"Well, Opal did," Mollie continued. "She spent her days here roaming the beaches, putting herself into trances, and performing healing rituals. But then, her behavior grew even more erratic and eccentric. She claimed that she was being psychically attacked. A few nights later, she was gone. Vanished.

"They found her body the next day, wrapped in a black cloak, surrounded by five candles. A knife was also discovered at the scene."

"Sounds like she was offered up as a sacrifice or something," Kate noted.

"Her official cause of death was exposure to the elements, but there are a fair few who, to this day, believe her death was supernatural."

"And has her ghost been spotted here?" Luke asked.

"Not as often as the monks. Or the nuns."

"The nuns?"

"Yes, the Iona Nunnery is just beyond the ferry docks and we have several visitors who report seeing the ghosts of the nuns in the graveyard."

"Oh man, we will definitely have to check that out," Luke grinned. "I'm thinking tonight after dinner."

"I'm in," Gail said.

"Sounds awesome," Peter agreed.

"Okay, so, just for clarification... you want us to hike back to the hostel for dinner... then hike back to the Nunnery... and then back to the hostel," Michael said.

"You got it, Mikey!" Luke exclaimed.

"Are you trying to kill me?"

Luke turned to Mollie.

"You'll have to forgive him. He's more of the indoor type."

"That's all right," Mollie told him. "Well then, are you ready to begin your tour of the Abbey?"

"I almost forgot that's why we're here," Peter laughed.

"There really is so much to see and to talk about. It's easy to get distracted," Mollie grinned.

The tour began with a brief introduction and acknowledgment of St. Oran's Chapel and the burial ground adjacent to the Abbey itself.

"That is supposedly where you'll find the remains of several Kings of Scotland, including Malcolm and Macbeth," Mollie explained.

"Oh, man, that's cool. Mikey, do you see any Kings?" Luke asked.

"Not at the moment," Michael replied.

Next, Mollie pointed out St. Martin's Cross, a great stone structure that still stood on its original site over twelve-hundred years after its construction. It seemed to Michael that the ancient wonder existed to watch over the entrance to the Abbey, and after all that the sacred site had endured, perhaps it needed a proper guardian.

Inside, Iona Abbey was far from extravagant. With walls of aged gray stones and rows of wooden chairs facing the altar, it was simple, very modest, but above all, it was peaceful. That was something Michael hadn't been expecting. But as he gazed around at the stone arches and antique candelabras, he felt an undeniable sense of reverence inside the sanctuary.

Kate seemed equally entranced.

"This is amazing," she whispered.

"Yeah, it is," Michael agreed.

"I don't know how to describe it... but there's just something... pure about this place."

"I feel it, too."

It was only then that Michael realized Luke and the rest of the team had already moved on with Mollie, leaving Kate and him alone in the nave. He was just about to ask her if she wanted to follow them when she spoke again.

"I wonder what it would be like to get married here." It was an innocent thought, a simple statement, but her words caught both of them off guard. Michael stopped dead in his tracks while Kate's eyes widened with what could only be described as minor alarm. "Not that I'm hinting at anything or trying to pressure you!" she declared, all in a rush. "I just... I was thinking out loud and I - "

"Do you want to?"

No!

Now it was Michael's turn to fret. This wasn't how it was supposed to happen! The question had slipped his lips as though it were nothing more than a mere afterthought... a curious whim. He didn't even have the ring.

But the way Kate was looking at him, her eyes so full of hope and love... There was no way he could look into those eyes and *not* ask her.

"Do I want to...?" she whispered, her voice shaking.

Michael took her hands and prayed to whatever deity happened to be listening that he wouldn't stammer. Or faint.

"Kate, I... I've been wanting to ask you something since the day we got here. Since the day I met you, actually," he confessed. "And this... this isn't at all how I pictured it. I wanted to ask you on a beach while we watched the sunset... or on a hill overlooking a castle. I'm completely unprepared right now - "

"Michael!" Kate exclaimed, choking out a laugh. "Just ask me."

And so, dropping down to one knee, he did as she said.

"Kate?"

"Yes?"

Deep breath. Deep breath.

"Will you marry me?"

Kate beamed at him, tears streaming down her cheeks.

"You know I will."

Then she pulled him back up to his feet and kissed him with such passion, Michael was all but certain that the walls around them would crumble.

CHAPTER TWENTY-THREE

"I have a ring for you," Michael said once Kate finally released him.

"You do?" She didn't know why, but that surprised her. Had he really been planning this all along? Was that why they were there?

"Yeah, but it's back at the hostel."

"What?" she laughed.

"I've had it for weeks and I've been carrying it around with me ever since... except for tonight," Michael said, heaving a defeated sigh.

"Oh, that's too funny," Kate snickered.

"I don't think it's funny," Michael remarked, but his smile absolutely gave him away.

"It's a little funny," Kate argued, wrapping her arms back around his neck. "So was this the plan all along?"

"No, this wasn't the plan at all! I wanted your proposal to be something magical, something really spectacular."

"You know you could have proposed to me in a parking lot and I still would have said yes."

"That's what Brink said," Michael grinned. But then, much to Kate's surprise, his face fell. "Oh, no. Brink."

"What?"

"I promised him that I wouldn't propose without him."

"You two *are* sort of a packaged deal. But I'm sure he'll understand."

"He made me swear on his grave."

"That's a little dramatic."

"Oh, and Luke!"

"He made you swear on Luke's grave, too?"

"No. Luke wanted to film it. He thought it would make for good ratings."

"You mean... I could have gotten engaged on *Cemetery Tours*?" Okay, *that* would have been cool.

"It was literally the first thing that Luke asked when I told him I wanted to propose to you."

"Well, he has always been pretty invested in our relationship," Kate acknowledged. "Is that why he asked us if we wanted to come to Scotland?"

"I actually asked him if we could come," Michael told her.

"You did?" Kate was stunned. "But you never ask Luke for *anything!*"

"I wanted it to be special," Michael admitted sheepishly.

"Well, you succeeded."

Engaged. They were *engaged*! Kate was so overwhelmed by joy, so enthralled with excitement, so consumed with love that she felt almost delirious. She was going to marry Michael. Michael was going to be her *husband*. The very thought made her heart sing.

Is this what it was like when Trevor proposed to me?

And just like that, the music in her heart was muted.

No! she scolded herself. *Don't do this to yourself. Not now. Not now.*

To her great and utter relief, her memories of that particular moment remained hidden and she was able to keep smiling for Michael.

"I love you, Katherine Avery," he told her, blissfully unaware of the war her mind kept trying to rage on her.

"I love you too, Michael Sinclair," she echoed. "If I could marry you tomorrow, I would."

Then, there in the company of saints and kings, she rose up on her tip-toes and kissed him again.

Michael couldn't believe it.

He did it.

It had happened so fast. He'd barely even had time to think about it. But it had happened, and despite it not going at all the way he'd hoped it would, he couldn't have been happier. And he couldn't wait to give her the ring.

Granted, there were still two miles of rural terrain to conquer before he would be able to do so. But in the end, he knew it would all be worth it.

"All right," Luke called everyone to attention once their tour of the Abbey ended and they'd all reconvened on the graveled pathway. "Now that we've checked that off the list, Pete and I are on our way to the market. Does anyone have any last-minute requests? Or would anyone like to join us?"

"Not even a little bit," Gail remarked.

"You took the words right out of my mouth," Hayes remarked.

"I'll go," J.T. volunteered.

"Mikey? Kate?" Luke asked.

"I think we're going to head back to the hostel," Kate said, taking Michael's hand and lacing her fingers through his. "I want to change. And maybe go for a walk on the beach."

"Well, don't wear yourselves out. Remember, we've got an investigation tonight," Luke said.

"Don't worry. We'll be ready," Kate assured him. Then, glancing up at Michael, she teased, "Well, *I'll* be ready."

"Oh, Mikey," Luke sighed. "One day, *one day*, I'm going to get you to admit that you actually enjoy this."

"Yeah. Good luck with that," Michael remarked.

"I don't think even *I* have that power," Kate laughed as she took a few steps up the road, pulling Michael along with her. "Come on, let's go."

"We're going to get dinner started as soon as we get back so don't wander too far!" Luke called after them.

"Oka-ay!" Kate sang back, effectively ending the conversation.

Of course, it didn't take long for Hayes to strike up a new one.

"So, you really don't enjoy this, Sinclair?" he asked.

Great. How did he expect him to answer that?

"Oh, you know..." Michael trailed off.

"No, I don't know. That's why I'm asking."

Michael resisted the urge to press his free hand to his temple. Leave it to Hayes to give him a headache on the happiest day of his life.

"I can think of better ways to spend an evening," he answered.

"What? Than running around chasing dead people in the dark?" Gail asked. "What could be better than that?"

"I don't know. Reading? Sleeping? Getting a root canal?"

"If you hate it so much, then why do you go along with it?" Hayes asked.

"I don't hate it. It's more that I'm still learning to accept it." Michael suspected Hayes was hoping to catch him off guard, to get him to finally admit that it was all an elaborate act.

"So basically, if it weren't for Rainer, you wouldn't be doing all of this."

"I wouldn't go looking for ghosts, no. But they'd still be there. They'd figure out a way to track me down." *They always do.*

"You know, I've got to hand it to you, Sinclair. You're a fascinating case."

It wasn't a compliment by any means, but it wasn't the least flattering thing that Hayes had ever said about him, either. Michael decided to consider it a win.

As soon as they arrived back at the hostel, Hayes excused himself to do some work while Gail announced, rather loudly, that she was going to take a nap. Michael couldn't say for sure, but he had a feeling her declaration was actually an invitation for Hayes to join her. Kate appeared to be harboring similar suspicions.

"You know, we should probably make ourselves scarce," Kate remarked. "Just in case."

"I think you might be right," Michael agreed. "But first, there's something I need to give you."

Kate's face broke into a broad, beautiful smile.

"I wasn't going to be the one to bring it up, but now that you have, yes, there is something you need to give me," she said, her eyes sparkling with light and love.

"Why didn't you want to bring it up?" Michael laughed.

"I didn't want to seem eager. Now let's go!" she exclaimed. Then she took off, all but dragging him through the hostel to their bedroom.

Once inside, Michael shut the door before crossing the small albeit cozy room to his side of the bed, where he'd stashed his suitcase. Hastily, with fumbling fingers and jittery nerves, he unzipped the front pocket and retrieved the black velvet box bearing the ring.

"So, how do you want me to do this?" he asked, making his way back to where she stood. "Do you want me to get down on one knee again? Or should I just give it to you?"

"Whatever you prefer. I'm going to marry you either way," Kate grinned.

"Oh, good. That makes this a *lot* easier." He was only sort of joking.

"Did you honestly think I was going to say no?"

"It was more that I was afraid I was going to ruin it somehow."

"You couldn't possibly ruin anything," Kate assured him.

"In that case..." Caught up in the rush and romance of the moment, Michael dropped back down onto one knee and opened the box. "Katherine Avery, I - "

"WHAT ARE YOU DOING!?"

Michael was so startled by the bratty ghost's sudden appearance that he almost fell over.

"Holy sh - Brink!"

"Brink!" Kate scolded. "You almost made my fiancé *curse* in the middle of my proposal!"

"You promised me! You swore *on my grave* that you wouldn't propose without me! And yet here you are!"

"Brink, please, let me explain - "

"Ugh, I wish I hadn't given up on trying to teach myself telekinesis! I would *Matilda* that ring right out of your treacherous hand!"

"I'm sorry - "

"I even helped you pick *out* the ring!"

"No, what you did was the opposite of help," Michael reminded him.

"He's upset, huh?" Kate asked.

"Honestly, I could have had a secret wife and she'd be pitching less of a fit right now."

"Brink, we really are sorry," Kate said.

"Tell her her words are hollow, just like my dead heart," Brink pouted.

"No, I'm not going to tell her that."

"Then go get one of Luke's walkie-talkie radio things and I'll tell her myself."

"Brink, come on. Can't you just be happy for us?"

"I don't want to be happy."

Michael rubbed his forehead. It was like dealing with a crabby toddler. Worse, actually. At least a toddler could be bribed with cookies or put down for a nap.

"You know, Brink, he still hasn't put the ring on my finger," Kate reminded him. "I haven't even gotten a good look at it yet."

Brink paused for a moment to take that into consideration.

"I guess she has a point," he finally conceded.

"Thank you," Michael sighed. Then, he turned back to Kate and presented her with the ring.

"Oh, my God," she breathed. "Oh, Michael. It's perfect."

"I hoped you would like it," he smiled.

"I love it!" she exclaimed. "And I love you."

"I love you - "

But before he could get the words out, she'd thrown her arms around his neck, nearly knocking him clear off his feet.

"Imagine how she would have reacted if you'd gone with one of the rings *I* picked out," Brink commented.

Michael didn't dignify that with a response.

They eventually did make it down to the beach, and it was even more magical than Kate could have imagined. The waters were as clear and vibrant as the summer sky, the sand as soft as clouds. Then there were the stunning formations of beach rock which seemed to both decorate and guard the sacred shores.

It would serve as the perfect backdrop for a few engagement pictures.

"Wait, really?" Michael asked as soon as she flipped her phone camera into selfie mode.

"Yes, really."

"But... I thought you wanted to come down here to explore and enjoy the scenery."

Kate rolled her eyes. She should have known he'd resist. Michael hated having his picture taken, though for the life of her, she couldn't understand why. He always looked so cute.

"I do, but I also want to remember this moment for the rest of our lives. So come on. Smile."

Begrudgingly, he obliged. Kate snapped five, ten, at least fifteen different pictures, and she could have easily taken at least a dozen more, but she hated to hold Michael hostage any longer than she already had.

"I think that's enough," she said. "Thank you."

"You're welcome," he grinned, leaning in to kiss her lips.

Acting almost entirely on instinct, Kate lifted her hand up and snapped one last selfie.

"Sorry. Couldn't resist. But look how beautiful we are!" she exclaimed, showing him the picture. "I think I'm going to have to share this one."

"Just don't post anything about being engaged yet. I still have to tell my mom. Oh, and Luke..."

"I thought you said Luke knew."

"He does, but he wanted to film it, remember?"

Kate thought for a moment.

"Well you know, we could always stage a proposal," she suggested. "Now that we're both in on it, we could probably come up with something worthy of those primetime ratings."

"Do you want to make Luke happy or do you just want to get engaged on television?" Michael teased. He knew her far too well.

"Both," she laughed.

And then it hit her.

That dreadful chill, like icy breath on the back of her neck. The pounding of her heart that had nothing to do with the love and elation she'd been experiencing mere moments before. It was a feeling she knew all too well, one that was impossible to ignore.

Somewhere, a ghost was watching them.

CHAPTER TWENTY-FOUR

"We're here on the mystic Isle of Iona. Now, I don't know how much you guys know about Iona, but this place... it's weird. At first, you think it's weird in a good way with all the beaches and old crosses and friendly neighborhood sheep herds. But then... you walk into the kitchen... and you find *this*."

Luke turned around to see Pete, who was either live-streaming or recording as he and J.T. labored away over a hot stove, preparing dinner for everyone.

"Ladies, and gentlemen, this is truly an astonishing sight," Pete continued, as he strolled on into the kitchen for a better angle. "So, what are you making, Luke?"

Never one to resist the spotlight, Luke channeled his inner celebrity chef and presented his dish.

"I am making oven-roasted asparagus," he answered. "Drizzled with olive oil and sprinkled with pepper and salt and a pinch of garlic. Just a pinch."

"And have you ever made this before?"

"No."

"Have you ever made anything before?"

"He can make a hell of a tequila sunrise," J.T. chimed in.

"That I can," Luke concurred. "We should have bought some tequila while we were at the market."

"We're in Scotland. They drink whisky here," J.T. reminded him.

"Then, we should have bought some whisky while we were at the market."

"We could have bought some at the Edinburgh Castle whisky shop, but we didn't. Because you wouldn't let us go," Pete complained.

"Well Pete, if you get thirsty, you could always sip on that *whine*," Luke commented. "Now if you'll excuse me, my asparagus is ready to roast."

"God, I hope you don't poison us," Pete remarked.

"I guess we'll find out, won't we?"

It was good, light-hearted fun. After spending so much time immersed in the dark history of the places that they investigated and being drained by the spirits that resided there, it was nice, and often times essential, to step back, let their guards down, and laugh.

Kate and Mikey appeared shortly thereafter, sporting windblown hair and sun-kissed cheeks.

"Oh my goodness, it smells *amazing* in here," Kate declared.

"Hungry?" Luke grinned.

"I'm *starving*."

"It's the salty air. It'll do that to you."

"No, I'm pretty much always hungry," she laughed. "Do you guys need any help?"

"Yeah, actually. Would you mind setting the table?"

"Not at all."

As Kate and Mikey set about retrieving plates from the cupboards and silverware from the drawers, Luke couldn't help but picture them a few years into the future, in a house of their own, married, maybe with a couple of kids running around. He had no idea if either of them even wanted kids, but he secretly hoped that they did. It would be fun to be Uncle Luke.

After dinner, which was exceptional if he did say so himself, they cleaned the kitchen, washed the dishes, and then they gathered in the living space while they waited for the sun to go down.

"So, Mikey, tell me. Have you seen any ghosts here?" Luke asked.

"Not yet," Michael answered. "Kate sensed one earlier, though."

"You did?"

"Yeah. While we were down at the beach," Kate answered.

"But Mikey, you didn't see it?"

"I was... distracted," he blushed.

"Yeah, right. *Distracted*," Pete winked. "We all saw the pictures."

"You already posted them?" Mikey asked Kate.

"We're cute," she shrugged.

The sun finally began to set an hour later, so they gathered up all of their equipment and set off back down the road to the nunnery. Hayes stayed behind, claiming that he still had a little bit of "work" to finish up. Luke didn't believe him for a moment, but for once, he wasn't going to argue. They didn't need his negative energy affecting the nuns.

By the time they arrived at their destination, a court of crumbling ruins, dusk had fallen and a strong wind had picked up, carrying in heavy clouds that obscured the stars.

"Do you think we should be out here?" Michael asked, gazing up at the ominous sky. "It looks like it might rain."

"Don't worry. We've got tarps and umbrellas to cover up the cameras," Luke assured him.

"As odd as it sounds, Luke, it's not the cameras I'm worried about."

"Well, I hate to break it to you, Mikey, but I think your hair is a lost cause with or without the rain."

Michael looked to Kate for support, but as usual, she just laughed.

The crew worked quickly setting up their equipment while Michael kept an eye out for ghosts. And it wasn't long before he spotted one.

She wasn't a nun. Or if she was, she didn't look like one. She was just an ordinary middle-aged woman dressed in a flowing white nightgown. She moved slowly around the garden surrounding the nunnery, her hands clasped together in prayer.

"Someone's here," Michael whispered to Kate.

"Where?"

"By those flowers over there."

Without another word, Kate darted away from him and over to where Luke was checking his spirit box and digital recorder.

"Hey. I need a camera," she told him.

"Why? Does Mikey see something?"

"Yeah."

"Excellent. Here."

She returned moments later with a digital point-and-shoot camera and an EMF detector. To his surprise, she handed him the camera.

"Here you go," she said.

"Wait... I get the camera?"

"You're the one who can see her," Kate reasoned.

"Right."

It felt strange, almost like an invasion of privacy, to point the camera so deliberately at the woman, but she didn't seem to notice. Maybe she was so used to strangers and their disruptive devices that she'd learned to ignore them. Or perhaps, like so many other spirits, she had grown accustomed to being ignored herself.

"Okay, we're ready," Luke announced in a somewhat hushed tone. "Have you been able to make contact yet?"

"No," Kate answered.

"I don't think she knows we're here," Michael added.

"Or she doesn't know that we know that she's here," Luke said. Then, he reached into his pocket, pulled out his digital recorder, and began rolling. "Hello? Is there someone here with us?" The woman didn't respond. "My name is Luke Rainer. Are there any ghosts here with us?" Still nothing. "Are you a nun?" Finally, he turned to Michael. "Anything?"

"No. It's like... she can't hear you," Michael answered.

"Do you think she's deaf?" Gail asked.

"Mr. Boots was blind," Peter reminded them.

"You know, I've just thought of something," J.T. said.

"What's that?" Luke asked.

"According to my research, this nunnery was established sometime in the thirteenth century. Scotland didn't become an English-speaking country until hundreds of years later."

"So it isn't that she can't hear is. It's that she can't understand us," Luke concluded.

"Does anyone speak Gaelic?" Gail asked.

"I can speak a little Klingon," Pete said.

"Well, that might come in handy the next time we're investigating a sci-fi convention."

"Guys, stop it. I'm trying to think," Luke snapped.

"I think the best we can hope for now is to try to capture her on camera," J.T. said. "And we'd better hurry, too. I just checked the weather radar and it's about to get pretty nasty."

"Okay, then. Here's what we're gonna do," Luke announced. "Kate, I'm going to have you get as close to her as you possibly can with that EMF detector. I'll film you. Gail, I want you on the thermal cam. Let's see if it can't pick up any unusual cold spots. Pete and J.T., keep rolling with the night vision cameras. And Mikey, take as many pictures as you possibly can. Fill up the memory card. I've got plenty. And if you can, try to get her from different angles, too. Who knows if and when she might show up."

And so, they set their plan into action. Michael tried his best with the point-and-shoot, but it was tricky. While he could easily see the nun with his own eyes, she didn't appear on the camera's tiny screen, making it difficult to know whether or not he was actually capturing her.

Although she must have known they were there, she never gave any indication that their presence bothered her. In fact, she seemed very much at peace there in her garden.

It wasn't until the first raindrops began to fall that Michael noticed any change in her behavior. As the weather worsened, the nun turned her face toward the sky, blinking away the rain even though it would have no real effect on her. Then, with one last silent prayer, she vanished into the night.

"She's gone!" Michael called out to his friends, hoping that they would be following her lead very, very shortly.

"You're sure?" Luke asked as the rain began falling in sheets.

"Does it even matter?" Gail hollered. "Come on, if we stay out here any longer, we're going to catch pneumonia!"

"You know, that's actually a myth - "

"Oh, my God, I so don't care! Let's go!"

No one else needed to be persuaded. Shielding the equipment with tarps, umbrellas, and even their own bodies, they fought their way against the wind and the rain all the way back to the hostel.

Finally, after two miserable miles, they reached their haven at the end of the road. Its windows glowed with warmth and comfort, and the sight alone filled Michael with such relief that he could have wept.

That relief, however, was short-lived. Because that's when he saw her: a wild woman with untamed hair, standing at the edge of the grassy hill overlooking the beach. The same beach where he had stood with Kate mere hours earlier.

She was the one who had been watching them before. Michael was sure of it.

"Michael, come on!" Kate called. She was already inside, where it was safe and dry.

With one quick glance back to make sure the ghost woman wasn't going to follow him, Michael hastened inside where Kate was waiting with two clean towels.

"Thanks," he shivered, suddenly very aware of how chilled he was. He was also soaked to the bone. And tired. God, he was so tired.

Kate could see it, too.

"Let's go get ready for bed," she murmured, her voice gentle and soothing.

Michael was so exhausted, he could only nod in response.

That night, Kate dreamed of a wedding.

Not just any wedding. *Her* wedding.

It was a beautiful spring day, perfect for an outdoor ceremony. The wedding garden was filled with the smiling faces of people she loved. She had never been happier... or felt more beautiful. Dressed in a gown of elegant lace and sparkling sequins and carrying a stunning waterfall bouquet of daylilies, carnations, and roses, she felt like a Princess in a fairy tale.

"You look just lovely, Pumpkin," her dad smiled, offering her his arm.

"Thank you, Daddy."

Then, the wedding march began.

Kate fought back tears as her groom turned to face her. His dark eyes lit up as soon as he saw her. Kate's heart swelled with love and anticipation. He was hers, now. He was her future. He was her forever.

Michael.

Beneath the floral arch, Michael reached out his hand as Kate's father presented her to him.

"Be good to her," Rex told him.

"I will, Sir," Michael promised.

Rex left them then, and suddenly, Kate realized that their officiant was nowhere to be seen.

But... that couldn't be right. Who would marry them? Curious, she looked around, hoping that someone would step forward to perform the ceremony.

Michael watched her with sympathetic eyes.

"He wanted to be here today," he told her.

"What?" she asked.

"He wanted to be with you."

"Who?" Kate asked.

Then, to her surprise, it began to snow. A frigid wind blew in from the north, carrying petals away from her bouquet. Kate gasped, frantic to stop them before she was left holding nothing but bare stems.

"What's happening?" she cried. "It's freezing!"

Screeeeeeeech!

CRASH!

Horrified by the sound of shrieking brakes and the distinct yet sickening crunch of a car collision. She turned to see the smoking wreckage of an automobile at the base of a tree just beyond the garden.

"Oh, my – Call 911!" she screamed, dashing to the scene as quickly as possible in a wedding dress.

When she reached the car, the door was jammed, and she had to rely on every ounce of strength and body weight that she possessed to open it. Yet, when she finally succeeded, the car was mysteriously empty.

"Oh, thank God," she sighed. No one had been hurt.

Weak with relief, she turned back to her groom and was pleasantly surprised to find where one man once stood, now there were two.

Finally, the officiant had deemed to show up.

Regaining her composure, she tucked a stray lock of hair behind her ear and made her way back down the aisle to

Michael. She smiled nervously, hoping that he would forgive her for just running off like that.

Then she glanced over his shoulder and made eye contact with the man standing behind him. And that's when her heart thudded to a stop.

A corpse stared back at her.

Pale, mangled, and covered in fresh blood, it was the man who'd died in the car crash. The one she had fought so desperately to save.

Trevor.

"*NO!*" she screamed.

"Kate! Kate!" Michael's voice echoed in her ear.

"No!" Kate cried out again, thrashing against her veil, which had somehow managed to wrap itself around her.

No... it wasn't her veil at all. It was bedsheets.

She was in bed. There hadn't been a wedding.

But there *had* been a car accident. And Trevor was still dead. And suddenly, Kate was sobbing so hard she could barely breathe.

"Kate," Michael whimpered. He sounded broken. "What is it? Please, tell me..."

"I remember him." The words were out before she could stop them.

"What?" Now his voice trembled with anguish.

"Not all of him," Kate clarified. "I... I don't remember his details. I couldn't tell you his middle name or his favorite book. But... there are moments. They've been coming back to me more and more. And now, I've just had a dream..." She couldn't tell him. It was too much.

"Oh, Kate..." he whispered, pulling her into his arms. "Why didn't you say something?"

"Because I didn't want to hurt you," she wept. "I love you so much..."

"I love you, too," he sniffled. Kate's heart broke all over again when she realized he was crying also.

"I'm sorry... I'm sorry..."

"Oh, sweetheart, no. You have no reason to be sorry. Please… don't apologize."

Several moments passed in silence as Michael held her tight and just let her cry. It was raw and heart-wrenching, but it was also very cathartic. Although those memories had left her devastated, she found the utmost comfort there in Michael's embrace.

But all of a sudden, his body language changed. His back stiffened. His arms tightened around her. She could feel his hot breath on her neck as he exhaled slowly.

"Michael?" She pulled away and looked up at him. "What is it?"

She didn't know why she'd asked. It was a question to which she already knew the answer.

Someone was with them inside their bedroom. And that someone was a ghost.

CHAPTER TWENTY-FIVE

Michael didn't sleep a wink the rest of the night.

"I remember him."

Those words... those horrible, awful, soul-shattering words echoed in his mind. Over and over and over.

"I remember him."

She said that the memories had been coming back gradually. She didn't mention when, specifically, but Michael had his suspicions. That afternoon on the Isle of Skye. That night at Dunadhar Castle. How could he have missed it? How could he not have known? He was supposed to be the one who loved and protected her above all others and he hadn't even been able to identify the source of her despair.

But Kate's confession wasn't the only thing that haunted him.

The wild woman was back. She'd been watching them all night.

Michael wasn't sure if she'd figured out that he could see her, but he was willing to bet that she had. Why else would she have stood steadfast by their bed into the odd hours of the morning?

Since he couldn't sleep, every once in a while, he would try to sneak a glance at her. She was young, probably in her early to mid-thirties, and she wore a black cloak wrapped around her body. He didn't have to wonder who she was.

Opal Murray. The occultist. No wonder she had taken such a keen interest in them.

Now if only she would lose interest. The sun was beginning to rise. Everyone would be waking up soon, including Kate.

Michael was thankful that she'd been able to fall back asleep. Her body needed to rest and her mind needed to heal.

God, why did she have to remember?

He didn't feel threatened by her memories of Trevor. Not in the least. He knew she loved him and believed with all his heart that she wanted to marry him. He just hated seeing her in so much pain. Although her memory loss had been a burden in many ways, it had also been a blessing. It had kept her from suffering the loss of someone she loved.

But now...

"The girl is in danger," Opal announced, her voice trembling.

Michael was so surprised by her sudden declaration that he let his guard down and looked up, directly into the ghost's wide gray eyes.

Busted, Michael scolded himself.

"What?"

"I need to cleanse her. Quickly, move away from her."

"No." He kept his voice quiet, but firm.

"Her soul is weary. She is vulnerable, susceptible to negative energy. And it is here. I can feel it. I need to cleanse her."

"You're not going to touch her," Michael snapped.

"Michael?" Kate murmured.

"Kate." His tone softened. "It's okay. You're okay."

"Who are you talking to?"

He hesitated.

"No one."

"She knows I'm here," the ghost told him. "You must tell her the truth. Tell her there is a dark energy and it is feeding off of her. The only way to save her is to let me heal her."

Michael ignored her.

"How are you feeling?" he asked Kate.

"My head hurts. But I'm okay," she answered. "How are you?"

"I'm doing all right." It was a halfhearted answer, one that wasn't altogether true, but for the moment, it needed to be. He needed to be strong for her.

"Tell her she needs to be cleansed! She must be set free!" Opal insisted.

"Did you get some rest?" Kate asked.

"A little." Another white lie.

And then, a miracle happened. She smiled.

"Good," she whispered, reaching up to run her fingers across his cheek. Then, she hoisted herself up onto her elbow, leaned forward, and kissed him tenderly on the mouth.

In that moment, Michael nearly forgot everything: his anxiety, his guilt, Kate's memories of Trevor, even the ghost who still stood, watching them with those strange, stormy eyes –

Knock, knock, knock!

"Mikey! Kate! Is everybody decent?" Luke's voice called from behind their closed bedroom door. "I sure as hell hope so because I'm coming in!"

Less than half a second later, the door swung open and Luke burst into the room with such an intense blast of energy that Opal vanished on the spot. And in that moment, Michael honestly couldn't say he blamed her.

"We got the most *amazing* evidence last night!" Luke exclaimed.

"You know, I've got to ask. What would you have done if we *hadn't* been decent?" Kate wanted to know.

"Did you not hear what I just said? We've. Got. Evidence! Not one, not two, but *three* amazing pictures. And Mikey, I owe it all to you."

"Hooray," Michael murmured into his pillow.

"Now granted, it's not a brick floating in midair or an intelligent EVP, but I think we're well on our way. I've already checked the forecast for tonight and we are in the clear. I'm going to send at least two or three of us back to the nunnery tonight, or I might send the whole team. It all depends on what we find on our hikes."

"Wait a minute, *hikes*? As in plural?"

"You bet, Mikey! We've got a lot of island to cover! So, come on, get up! Time's a-wastin'!"

Then, he turned around and left the room, just as abruptly as he'd entered.

Michael, meanwhile, could only groan.

"Maybe next time we travel, we make it just the two of us," he muttered to Kate.

"I wouldn't object to that," Kate replied, running her fingers through his hair. "Where would you want to go?"

"I don't know. Somewhere sunny, I think. Definitely somewhere that isn't known for its ghosts."

"So, Australia, maybe? Or Fiji?"

"Hawaii… The Bahamas…"

"The Galapagos Islands…"

"The Galapagos Islands?" Michael laughed.

"Yes!"

"You want to visit the Galapagos Islands?"

"Are you kidding? I'd love to visit them. They have tortoises there."

"They have tortoises at the zoo," Michael reminded her.

"Irrelevant."

"So, is that where you want to go on our honeymoon? Somewhere you can see wild tortoises?"

"That's not my *only* criteria," Kate teased. But then, her eyes softened.

"What is it?" Michael asked.

"It's nothing. I…" Kate took a deep breath and exhaled slowly. "I just… found myself wondering where I'd been planning to go with Trevor."

"Kate." Michael sat up so he could face her directly. "You know you can talk to me about him, right?"

"I know," Kate whispered. "The thing is that I... I don't want to. I don't want to talk about him. I don't even want to think about him. Because the more I think about him, the more I might start to remember..."

It was then that Michael felt his heart breaking. Not for himself, but for Kate. And, oddly enough, for Trevor. Michael didn't know if Trevor could see them or hear them from wherever he was, but he could only imagine how painful it would be to hear the woman that he loved announce that she didn't want to remember him.

He had no words of comfort for her. He could only reach out for her, hold her, be there for her. And he hoped, for the moment at least, that that was enough.

"You know, if you want to stay in today, we can," Michael told her.

"No. I need to get out. It'll be good for me. It'll be good for *us*."

Michael couldn't imagine how another day of aching legs and blistering feet could possibly be good for him, but he wasn't about to mention that. He was going to support Kate... even if he was barely able to support himself.

"Today is a great day, isn't it? Isn't today a great day?" Luke proclaimed as he led them through the open fields of Iona. "I'm telling you guys, this is what life's about. Fresh air, sunshine, the spirit of adventure..."

"And the spirits of the dead," Peter quipped.

"Death is a part of life," Luke reasoned. "Isn't that right, Hayes?"

"It was a smudge on a camera lens, Rainer," Hayes grumbled.

"Wrong. It was a full-bodied apparition of a nun who has been haunting these grounds for centuries. Whose body lies buried beneath this island's very soil yet whose spirit lives on to this day."

"Your companion's fascination with death is troubling," Opal warned, falling into step beside Michael. "He seeks answers that he cannot possibly understand, and in doing so he opens himself up to otherworldly attacks and potentially life-threatening attachments."

Michael didn't respond. He didn't even acknowledge her. Instead, he kept his gaze fixed and focused, hoping that if he ignored her, she would take the hint and leave him alone.

It didn't seem to be working.

"He must know that seeking to breach the natural barriers between realms is not a practice to be taken lightly... even for those of us already possessing the gift of clairvoyance. It is a dangerous path to follow, one that has consumed and claimed many souls who have sought to conquer it."

Michael scrunched up his face into a grimace. Did she honestly expect him to understand a word of what she was saying?

"There are dark forces alive and at work in this world and it is our responsibility as gatekeepers to - "

"Wait a minute. As what?"

"Gatekeepers. Those who serve to protect the living from the dead. The guardians of the veil between worlds."

Of course. It was nonsense. Michael should have known better than to ask. He couldn't imagine there were many ghosts out there who would take him seriously as a guardian or a defender. They usually saw him as more of an errand boy.

There was, however, something else that had piqued his interest.

"What do you mean by 'the veil between worlds?'" he asked. "Ever since we got here, people have been talking about this island being a veil or a thin place and I have no idea what that's supposed to mean."

"Imagine, if you will, a door that can only be opened from one side. Now logically, once you pass through that door, it can never be opened again. *Unless* you happen upon a thin place. Then, it is possible for the door to open both ways."

"So, are you saying that it might be possible to reach someone who's already crossed over?"

"It is very possible."

Their conversation had carried them to the base of a hill where the rest of his companions were in the midst of setting up for a picnic lunch.

"Hey," Kate greeted him with a bright smile. "How are you holding up? Are you okay?"

"Oh yeah, I'm fine," he assured her despite being fairly certain he would be needing braces on both knees for the rest of his life.

"Good," she grinned and kissed him on the cheek.

"Mikey, there you are!" Luke exclaimed. "I was beginning to think we'd lost you."

"No, I was just... going at my own pace," he answered awkwardly. No one needed to know about his conversation with Opal.

"Well, at your age, that's understandable."

Oh, the age jokes were back. Super.

"Luke, I don't know how to break it to you, but you are *still* five years older than me."

"Creaky joints speak louder than birth certificates, Mikey."

"That makes no sense."

Meanwhile, the rest of the group snickered into their sandwiches as they all settled in for lunch. Kate, of course, seemed particularly tickled, and for that, Michael was thankful. After a harrowing night and an equally trying morning, he needed to see her smile.

That smile, unfortunately, was short-lived. She'd no sooner pulled out her phone than the laughter faded and an unsettling look of dismay and bewilderment moved in to take its place.

"What is it?" Michael asked her.

"It's a text message from Gavin."

"Is everything okay?"

"No," she answered. Then, she looked up and turned dour hazel eyes on Hayes. "You wrote another article?"

And just like that, a tense and uncomfortable silence descended upon the group as all gazes fell on Hayes. Not at all intimidated by their collective glare, he simply shrugged.

"News travels fast."

"What is it about?" Gail asked. "Is it about us?"

"Psychic or Psychosis? The Disturbing Case of Michael Sinclair." Kate read through gritted teeth. Michael realized with a start that she was fighting back tears. "What is this?"

"An analysis," Hayes responded.

"*Nestled amidst the hazy mountains and lush forests of the Scottish Highlands, Dunadhar Castle stands, frozen in time,*" Kate read. "*Constructed in the early fourteenth century, it is an idyllic setting for the fantasies and love stories with which so many have come to associate it. But Michael Sinclair would have you believe it to be home to something far more sinister.*

"*In the wake of my previous article's viral success, I was invited to spend some time with Michael Sinclair and a few of his friends while they "investigated" the supposed ghosts of Scotland. I expected to find an elaborate charade or perhaps a bag of magic tricks. The truth, unfortunately, is far more troubling.*

"*Michael Sinclair does, in fact, hear voices, but they are not the voices of the dead. They are products of his own mind, a sad but telling symptom of the same mental illness that claimed the life of his older brother, Jonathan, the summer before Michael's sophomore year of college.*"

Before he realized what was happening, Michael was on his feet, glowering down at Hayes, and seething with fury.

"How did you know that?" Michael asked, his voice trembling. He'd never been quick to anger, but hearing his brother's name, knowing that Hayes was using his illness, his death, his memory as a means to discredit him... it was more than he could bear. "*How* did you know that?"

"Michael, you had a brother?" Gail asked gently. But Michael was so livid, he could barely form a coherent thought.

"I want you to answer me *right now*," he demanded, his attention still fixed on Hayes. "*How* did you know about Jonathan?"

"I researched you. It really isn't that hard," Hayes admitted. Though, for the first time since Michael had met him, he sounded unsure of himself and of his actions.

"And you thought that it was *okay* to invoke my dead brother's illness to... what? To prove that none of it's real? That you're smarter than the rest of us?"

"I was *worried* about you," Hayes argued. "You really can't fault me for that. Especially when I'm not the only one."

"What does *that* mean?"

"It means that Kate worries about you, too. Has she ever told you that? Because she didn't seem to have a problem telling me."

"What are you talking about? I never said *anything* to you!" Kate insisted.

"Yes, you did. That night at the castle, remember? The staircase?"

"That's what you have to go on? A conversation that lasted, what? Thirty seconds?" Kate asked.

"Well, apparently it was enough for him to cite you in the article," J.T., who appeared to have pulled it up on his phone, remarked.

"What?" Kate exclaimed.

"*Michael Sinclair is a very sick man, and it is as apparent to those closest to him as it is to me. Even his longtime girlfriend, Katherine Avery, who suffers from a neurological condition herself, admits that she worries about him constantly.*"

"That's not what I meant and you know it, you arrogant son of a bitch," Kate growled.

"Look, I understand that you all want to make me out to be the villain of the piece," Hayes announced, rising to defend himself. "But you've misinterpreted my intentions. By writing and publishing this article, I was hoping that it might push you to finally get the help that you need. Or at least, force the people around you to accept that they can't keep enabling you and that they need to help you seek professional counsel. Will you really condemn me for that?"

"I will absolutely condemn you! You're derailing my life for - " But before he could finish, a heavy drowsiness swept over him, leaving his vision blurred and his body swaying.

"Peace, Michael," a woman's voice echoed inside his muddled mind. "You are feeding the darkness."

Opal.

"What... what are you..." he tried to ask, but she had all but drained him of the energy to speak.

"Do not despair. I am here to help you, remember?"

He couldn't fight her. He couldn't stop her. He could only watch with eyes that refused to focus as Opal confronted Hayes, her arms outreached, her hair flying wildly with the wind.

Michael tried to run to him, but it was no use. He stumbled once, twice, before collapsing into a heap onto the ground.

From somewhere far off in the distance, he heard someone call his name.

And then, the world around him faded to black.

CHAPTER TWENTY-SIX

When Michael opened his eyes again, he was back in the hostel. The sun hung low in the sky and he realized just how late it must have been.

Kate was there with him, reading a book in a chair next to the bed. She glanced up, however, when she sensed him stirring.

"Hey," she smiled, setting her book aside. "How are you feeling?"

"We seem to be asking each other that a lot recently," Michael remarked. "What happened?"

"I was hoping you could tell me," she responded. "Because whatever it was, it affected both you and Hayes."

"It was Opal," Michael explained. "Opal Murray. The girl that Mollie told us about."

"The one who was studying the occult?" Kate gasped.

"She's the one who's been watching us. She... seems to think we're cursed or something."

"Well, with Hayes and his garbage, she might have a point."

"Is he... you know... okay?" Considering the harsh words and ill intentions they'd exchanged just moments before Opal's intervention, Michael felt almost hypocritical asking about Hayes' well-being. But he needed to know.

"He's a little shaken up, I think. But he's fine. Gail was in with him earlier."

"Where is she now?"

"She went with Luke and the guys back to the nunnery. They seemed to think that was their best bet at capturing more evidence."

"You didn't want to go with them?"

"I wanted to stay here and take care of my fiancé," she grinned. "And since we're on the topic, you must be starving."

It wasn't until she mentioned it that Michael became aware of a hollow ache in his empty stomach.

"I could eat," he acknowledged.

"Let me see what we've got," Kate said, leaning over to kiss his lips before she left the room.

As soon as she was gone, Michael threw back his covers and swung his legs over the side of the bed. His whole body felt heavy, as though he had been drugged. He had a feeling that he was experiencing what Luke would call a "paranormal hangover."

Resisting the temptation to lie back down, he pulled himself up onto his feet and ventured, rather shakily, out of the room. He had no desire to speak to Hayes, but he knew that was where he was headed.

He found him in his bedroom, sitting in a chair next to the window, watching the sunset. Michael knocked softly on the open door before letting himself in. It came as no surprise that Hayes wasn't exactly thrilled to see him.

"What do you want, Sinclair?" he grumbled.

"Kate told me what happened. I wanted to see if you were all right."

"You care?"

"Well, no, not really. But I still wanted to make sure."

"If it clears your conscience, I'm fine."

"Well that's... good."

"Is it?" Hayes asked, turning to face him. "You don't sound so sure."

"No offense, but you're not exactly my favorite person."

"Believe me, I'm well aware."

"You know, I can handle criticism and I can handle doubt. I really don't care one way or another if you believe me or if you keep writing your articles. It's when you make it personal... when you drag Kate into it... or share private details about my brother... That's when I - "

"I saw her," Hayes cut him off.

"You... what?" Michael asked.

"I... saw her," Hayes repeated, this time begrudgingly, as though he resented before forced to speak the words twice.

"Who?"

Hayes heaved a heavy sigh.

"I don't know."

"What did she look like?" Michael asked slowly. He didn't want to jump to any conclusions. Because it was impossible. There was no way that Hayes had seen Opal.

Was there?

"Why should I tell you? So you can have some ill-gotten sense of validation?"

"Pale skin? Wide gray eyes? Dark, frizzy hair?" Michael watched as the bitter, hardened look on Hayes' face gave way to one of fear and uncertainty. "Black cloak?"

"That doesn't prove anything," he hissed.

"You're right. It doesn't," Michael agreed. "Still... you believe that you saw her."

"I believe in facts. In logic. And logic dictates that I can't have seen a woman who wasn't there."

"So, by your reasoning, the only logical explanation is that she *was* there."

Still, Hayes resisted.

"I don't know if I'm ready to accept that," he admitted.

"That's okay," Michael assured him, turning to leave. "Take your time."

"Sinclair," Hayes called after him. Michael glanced back at him. "I uh... I'm sorry. Not for writing the articles, necessarily. But for what I wrote about your brother. That was too far, and I apologize. I've taken it down."

"I appreciate that," Michael said. "Thank you."

"You're welcome. And now that I've said my peace, I'm going to pack up and I'm going to take my leave."

"You're not going to Stirling?"

"No. This isn't my world. It's yours. And as far as I'm concerned, I've seen quite enough of it."

"Well, if you ever have any questions or need someone to talk to… I'm sure I'd be able to find a medium willing to take you on."

"Oh, and here I thought we were about to have a moment," Hayes remarked with a wry grin. "Take care of yourself, Sinclair."

"You too, Caleb."

They spent their last day in Scotland investigating the ghosts of Stirling, a beautiful and historic city nestled in the very heart of the country. Their first stop was the Wallace Monument, a grand and majestic tower commemorating William Wallace's defeat of the English at the Battle of Stirling Bridge.

"So, are we looking for the ghost of Braveheart?" Peter asked as they made their way up the grueling staircase to the top of the tower.

"Unfortunately, we'd have to go all the way to Ardrossan Castle to find him," Luke answered. "We're just here to pay our respects."

"He could have mentioned that… *before* we started climbing," Michael huffed to Kate.

"Look at it this way. You're getting your cardio in."

"I've done… more cardio on this trip… than I have… in my entire life."

As much as he complained, however, he had to admit the view from the top of the monument was pretty spectacular. Far and wide, he could see the rolling green hills and low-hanging clouds, the city itself and the Firth of Forth.

"I think I'm going to miss this place," Kate sighed, resting her head against Michael's shoulders.

"We can always come back," Michael told her.

"True. And maybe by then, you'll be my husband," she grinned.

"You know," Michael murmured, lowering his voice. "I still need to propose to you for Luke."

"Yes, you do. I want to be able to wear my engagement ring."

"What do you think? Should I do it here?"

"No, this is a memorial. How about later on this afternoon when we go to the castle?"

"Sounds perfect," Michael said, taking her hand and toying gently with her fingers. Then he asked, "How are you? Are you... doing okay?" They hadn't discussed Trevor since the morning before on Iona, but Michael knew that his memory still weighed heavily on Kate's mind.

"Yeah, I'm fine." *For now.* The words were unspoken, but they were there. "I think I'm more afraid than anything. Afraid of how much it will hurt to *really* remember what it was like to love him. What if... what if it destroys me? I love the person I am now, the person I am when I'm with you. What if remembering him changes that?"

"It won't," Michael promised her, though his assurance was tinged with doubt.

"I just hope it's over. I hope that my brain decides enough is enough and goes back to harboring all those memories," Kate said.

"What if you could talk to him?" Michael asked.

"But... I thought you said he'd moved on."

"He did. But something Opal said to me on Iona made me wonder if..." he trailed off. Maybe he shouldn't mention it. He didn't want to tease her with ideas that stemmed from the ramblings of a madwoman. But it was too late.

"If what?" Kate asked.

"If maybe there was a way to reach them... the ones who've crossed over."

"But how?"

"I don't know. It's probably nonsense. But she said something about thin places like Iona being like a door..." He ran a hand through his hair and shook his head. "Like I said, I don't know. But it might be something to look into when we get home."

"You would do that?" Kate asked.

"Yeah, I would," Michael answered. "I would do anything for you."

Then, he pulled her in and kissed her mouth as the brisk Scottish wind danced around them.

Their journey ended in the courtyard of Stirling Castle. As the sun began its long descent and the ghost of a noble Highlander looked on from the castle bridge, Michael took Kate's hand and asked, "Ready?"

"You already know the answer," she grinned, her eyes sparkling with love and mischief.

Then, Michael signaled to Luke and the rest of the crew before turning back to Kate. It was show time. "So, you know, while we're here... I have something that I've been meaning to ask you."

"Oh, really?"

It was too much. Michael couldn't help but laugh.

"Come on, Mikey! You've got this!" Luke called from the sidelines.

"Thanks, Luke," Michael replied, grateful that his friend still had no idea that this second proposal was all an act.

"Better get it right this time," Brink grumbled. He'd gone out of his way to make it clear to Michael that he was going to be bitter about having missed the real proposal for years to come.

"I'll forgive you on one condition," Brink had said to him the night before. "You let me go with you on your honeymoon."

"Yeah, that's a hard no," Michael had responded.

"Then prepare to suffer the consequences."

As far as Michael was concerned, Brink could do his worst as long as he waited until they got back home to Dallas.

Back in the moment, looking into Kate's eyes as she waited for him to speak the words they'd rehearsed at least a dozen times, Michael felt remarkably at peace. For once, he was certain that everything was as it should be.

Of course, he knew the feeling couldn't last. There would always be another challenge to face, another heartbreak to withstand, another ghost to encounter. But Michael was confident he could weather at all… as long as he could be with Kate.

"I think I've known since the very first moment I met you that I was going to fall in love with you. Before, there really hadn't been a whole lot in life that made sense to me. But then, there you were and suddenly, everything seemed right."

Even though she knew exactly what he was going to say, Michael could see that Kate was fighting back tears. He realized then that he was as well.

"Kate," he continued, "Meeting you, falling in love with you, is the best thing that has ever happened to me. And I want nothing more than to love you and protect you and just be with you for the rest of our lives."

Finally, he dropped down onto one knee and presented her with the ring.

"Katherine Elaine Avery, will you marry me?"

Fighting back tears, Kate clasped her hand to her mouth and nodded.

"Yes, I will," she beamed.

Then, as the *Cemetery Tours* crew and a small crowd of onlookers burst into applause, Michael took her left hand and at long last, slipped the sparkling diamond ring onto her third finger.

AUTHOR'S NOTE

Hey, y'all!

Wow, thank you so much for sharing in another adventure with Michael, Kate, Luke, and of course, Brink. I hope this one was worth the wait.

First of all, I'd like to apologize for taking so long with this installment, but I wanted to make sure I got it right. My characters deserve that, and more importantly, you deserve that. I also wanted to make sure that I was accurately paying homage to Scotland, her history, and her ghosts. I spent countless hours researching Greyfriars Kirkyard, George Mackenzie, The Edinburgh Vaults, Nessie, The Isle of Iona, and everywhere and everything in between. Even though I've been to Scotland and visited many of these places, I didn't have the opportunity to delve into their pasts, their stories. I spent a whole five minutes in Greyfriars Kirkyard, not nearly enough time to fully appreciate its haunted history. Now, after writing *Lost Souls*, I can't wait to go back and visit the Black Mausoleum. See if I can't catch a glimpse of the real *Bluidy* Mackenzie.

That's something else I wanted to mention. Several of the ghosts in this book are based on actual hauntings and actual experiences. Of course, I'm using them in a fictional setting, but I think it's only right to acknowledge that many of them do exist (if you believe in ghosts, that is). Flora Colville is purely fictional, but she was inspired by the many innocent young women prosecuted and tortured as witches. Her castle, Dunadhar Castle, is also a figment of my imagination. In fact, it was a setting I created for another book, *Trashy Romance Novel* (available on Amazon!). I figured it was too great a castle to let go to waste.

For real though, go read *Trashy Romance Novel*. It's won awards and everything.

The other fictional ghost I wanted to mention is Opal Murray. You see, her story is actually based on the true and very mysterious account of a woman named Netta Fornario. She, like Opal, was a young occultist who passed away on the sacred Isle of Iona. I wanted to include her, but I didn't want to impugn her name or disrespect her in any way. George Mackenzie is another case entirely. By all historical accounts, this guy was a jerk. If any of his descendants are out there, I apologize. I'm sure you're awesome.

Again, thank you all so much for reading *Lost Souls* and for sticking with me while I took my time getting it out. I promise I won't make you wait nearly as long for Book Five.

WORK'S CITED

Banks, Peet. "Lady Janet Douglas." The Paranormal Guide. 2013.
http://www.theparanormalguide.com/blog/lady-janet-douglas

Bartlett, Amanda. "Ghostly Encounters in the Edinburgh Vaults."
The University of Iowa International Programs. Iowa City,
Iowa. June, 2014.
https://international.uiowa.edu/news/ghostly-encounters-edinburgh-vaults

Croal, Alice. "Iona: The Dark History of a Small Scottish Island."
Urban Ghosts. Urban Ghosts Media. July, 2014.
https://www.urbanghostsmedia.com/2013/07/iona-the-dark-history-of-a-small-scottish-island/

Harper, Jim. "Mackenzie Poltergeist in Greyfriars." Historic
Mysteries. Historic Mysteries: A Net Inceptions Project.
2018.
https://www.historicmysteries.com/mackenzie-poltergeist-greyfriars/

Haughton, Brian. "Occult Mystery on Iona - The Strange Case of
Netta Fornario." Mysterious People. Brian Haughton. 2004.
http://www.mysteriouspeople.com/Occult_mystery.htm

Lamkin, Virginia. "The Ghost of Lady Janet Douglas." Seeks
Ghosts. VLamkin. April, 2012.
https://seeksghosts.blogspot.com/2012/04/ghost-of-lady-janet-douglas.html

Matthews, Dana. "People Won't Stop Fainting in Greyfriars
Kirkyard, One of the World's Most Haunted Cemeteries."
Week in Weird. Planet Weird. August, 2016.

http://weekinweird.com/2016/08/01/people-wont-stop-fainting-in-greyfriars-kirkyard-one-of-the-worlds-most-haunted-cemeteries/

McDonald, Gillian. "How A Sceptical Scientist Tried to Prove That Edinburgh Castle was Haunted." The Essential Daily Briefing. iNews. October, 2017. https://inews.co.uk/inews-lifestyle/travel/edinburgh-castle-haunted/

Nugent, Addison. "Exposed to the Elements: A Strange 1920s Death on the Scottish Island of Iona." Mental Floss. September, 2018. http://mentalfloss.com/article/555841/strange-1920s-death-iona-scotland-nora-emily-fornario

Orr, Hayley. "13 Haunted Places in Scotland That Will Give You the Creeps." Visit Scotland: The Blog. Visit Scotland. October, 2017. https://www.visitscotland.com/blog/scotland/haunted-sites/

Strochlic, Nina. "Welcome to the Most Haunted Graveyard in the World. Safety Not Guaranteed." The Daily Beast: What a World. The Daily Beast Company, LLC. October, 2013. https://www.thedailybeast.com/welcome-to-the-most-haunted-graveyard-in-the-world-safety-not-guaranteed?ref=scroll

Wagner, Stephen. "The Ghosts of Edinburgh Castle." ThoughtCo. Dotdash. July, 2018. https://www.thoughtco.com/the-ghosts-of-edinburgh-castle-3572726

"Edinburgh Vaults' Haunted History." Travel Channel. The Travel Channel, LLC. 2019. https://www.travelchannel.com/shows/ghost-adventures/articles/edinburgh-vaults-haunted-history

"The History of the Loch Ness Monster." History of Scotland. Historic UK, Ltd. England. https://www.historic-uk.com/HistoryUK/ HistoryofScotland/The-Loch-Ness-Monster/

ACKNOWLEDGEMENTS

As always, thank you to my Lord and Savior for your love, your blessings, and your guidance.

Thank you to my amazing parents, Susie and David, for your constant support and for taking care of my kitties while I'm out of town.

Thank you to my sister (and my manager!), KJ, for not giving up on me and for continually nagging me to get this book finished already. It finally happened!

Thank you to my friends, Hannah, Jessica, Aïda, Jalitza, Amanda, Ashley, and Stephen for listening to me, encouraging me, and honestly, for giving me something to talk about other than this book.

Thank you to my colleagues, my fellow writers, including but not limited to James William Peercy (*The Wall Outside*) and his amanuensis, Claudette, Miracle Austin (*Boundless*), Terri R. Malek (*My Path to Omega*), Cody Wagner (*The Gay Teen's Guide to Defeating a Siren*), April L. Wood (*Winter's Curse*), Kendra L. Saunders (*Dating an Alien Popstar*), Sarah MacTavish (*Firebrand*), Susie Clevenger (*Where Butterflies Pray*) and her husband, Charlie, and so, so, so many others! Thank you for your guiding light and your love!

And finally, thank you to my beautiful, wonderful, amazing readers. There are far too many of you to list, but I'd like to at least mention Honor, Morgan, Natalie, Cassandra, Marine, Kaylin, Sandra, Lindsey, Marialena, Arnild, Tamar, Christina Candice, Camile, Prar, John, … I love you all! You mean the world to me!

Oh! And a special shout-out to the REAL Bill (our bus driver) and Alistair (our Edinburgh tour guide) from my own journey to Scotland. And a shout-out to Charlie, our tour guide from Iona, as well. Even though he's technically not in this book, if you've read *Boy Band*, the character of Oliver is totally based on him!

© 2017 by Fervent Images – Tim Malek

JACQUELINE E. SMITH is the award-winning author of the
CEMETERY TOURS series, the BOY BAND series, and
TRASHY ROMANCE NOVEL. A longtime lover of words,
stories, and characters, Jacqueline earned her Master's Degree
in Humanities from the University of Texas at Dallas in 2012.
She lives and writes in Dallas, Texas.

Made in the USA
Monee, IL
22 September 2021